Pasiphae

First published in the United Kingdom in 2000 by

Dewi Lewis Publishing
8 Broomfield Road
Heaton Moor
Stockport SK4 4ND
+44 (0)161 442 9450

All rights reserved

The right of Peter Huby to be identified as
author of this work has been asserted
by him in accordance with the
Copyright, Designs and Patents Act 1988

Copyright ©2000
For the text: Peter Huby
For this edition: Dewi Lewis Publishing
Front cover photograph: Peter Huby

ISBN: 1-899-235-87-6
Printed and bound in Great Britain by
Biddles Ltd, Guildford and King's Lynn

1 3 5 7 9 8 6 4 2

Pasiphae

Peter Huby

DEWI LEWIS
PUBLISHING

1

The bull is in a blue black slab of shade. It stands like a cottage or a cart, immobile, too big to be a breathing creature. In the inky prism of shadow the white, orange blotched flanks glimmer. The sand of the bull court rages white in the afternoon sun. In the gloom an ear moves, slightly.

It is the quiet time of day. A solitary servant walks flickering behind the pillars of the colonnade in and out of darkness: oiled skin, black crimped hair. Bare feet make a small business-like sound on the stone pavement. The palace is silent. In high airless rooms there is slack flesh and slow breathing. The sleepers have departed to other places and the bodies of the absent dreamers breathe sunkenly. A bead of sweat breaks into a rivulet. A dream rises to the surface like leviathan out of the void and momentary flinching animates the closed eyes. Fingers work.

Across the sandy court, beneath a fringed parasol the queen is watching the bull. Like the bull she is barely to be seen in the deep shadow. She begins to turn and a white bar of sunlight strikes the mole flecked skin, the gilded nipples, the bullion encrusted hoops of her skirt.

The boy holding up the heavy parasol is fixed in his anxiety to hold the queen within its cylinder of shade. The heavy beaded fringes of the royal parasol swish audibly. His thin arms cry out for release. The queen turns and addresses the darkness behind her. Nipples, navel, flash in the sun.

"Speak."

"It's like a house. Have you thought how heavy it is?"

"Is it possible?"

"I don't know, perhaps. I don't know."

"We'll watch it with the cows. I always watch it, with the cows. You must watch too. Tomorrow, and perhaps you will tell me then if it is possible."

2

The workshop is in the shipyards, an echoing cavern of a place. Inside its vaulted space the ribs of antique boats are piled hugely against the dim walls, half lost beneath the rubble and debris of centuries. Sails and cordage hang, fragile with age, in the half dark overhead. High up, a zigzag crack in the masonry, a relic of earthquakes, lets in a jagged lightning bolt of daylight. Seen from within, the doorway is a tiny rectangle of brilliant sunshine. Improbably, the painted prow of a ship passes by within its frame. The painted eye is like the moving eye of a dragon. Beyond the ship, the sea.

It is noonday. Just within the doorway an old man dozes, but when the fisherman's wife steps inside with her basket he does not wake. She smiles and passes into the long gloomy workshop. Daedalus is not there. The whole place is a midden, she thinks, as she picks her way past the piled chaotic workbenches. Every surface overflows: tools, dried up paint, brushes, discarded timber, jumbled bolts of cloth, grey with dust, buckets of dead flowers, rubbish of every type. A line of jointed wooden figures as tall as a man hang from a rail, like victims of an execution. The forge is cold. It stands on its cone of ash, surrounded by stacks of charcoal and a sprawl of ingots. The great leather bellows hang like lungs. She passes through a deep carpet of white woodshavings beneath a high ship's prow newly carved in the likeness of a dolphin. Above her head she notices a sort of bright sail, coloured silk stretched over a frame of lashed willow wands. It hangs gaudily over the ruinous workbenches.

Daedalus comes in through a doorway behind her, a doorway recently broken through from an adjacent warehouse. It is a ragged hole into darkness. Bricks and rubble are piled to one side of it. The fisherman's wife starts, clutching her chest.

"You made me jump. I didn't know there was a door there."

"There wasn't. It's new. It's not a door, it's a hole."

"What's that? That's new too."

She gestures up to the bright silk wing overhead.

"It's a kite."

"A what?"

"Come. I'll show you. You'll like this."

She follows him through the clutter to the far end of the place. He takes off the bar and pushes open a double door, letting in a dazzle of blue sea and blue day. She laughs out loud. The sky is full of white and red and green, a dozen kites swooping and bridling against the cobalt noon, a falling and climbing forest of colour. She begins to laugh tearfully out of pure pleasure.

"Here. Feel the wind."

He unfastens one of the kite-strings from the long rail at the water's edge to which they are tied and passes her the ball of twine. She holds it clenched in her hands as it tugs like something live, like a fish in the wind.

"Let it out. Let it go a little."

She begins hesitantly to uncoil the twine, allowing the red kite to inch higher and higher, out beyond its neighbours until it dances, a mere scintillation of scarlet against the dark blue vault of the day. The twine arcs from her hands, losing itself to the eye but she feels the fierce life of the sky in her arms. After a little while he takes the twine from her and ties it again to the rail. She unpacks the food from the basket she has brought and they sit in the shaded doorway to eat, squinting out at the horizon. He crunches the little red fish entire and tears the bread with his teeth. He spits out olive stones, trying to get them over the edge of the harbour wall and into the water. She takes the olive stones from her mouth with her fingers and throws them neatly into the water. Beyond the weaving kites, gulls drift, motes of white, tiny, abstract. She gazes upward, shading her eyes with her hand.

"They're lovely. What did you say they were called?"

"Kites, that's the word the sailors use. They're not new. They're not my invention, I don't think. In the East they have them in the shape of eagles. They use them to scare the birds from the crops, or so I was told, but then sailors will tell you anything."

He chooses a peach from the basket. Juice runs down his chin as he sinks his teeth into the soft flesh.

"Such a thing could carry a man, if it were big enough."

3

Noon. There is a momentary flickering against the sunlit doorway. He looks up from his work and sees her enter the workshop carrying the basket. She comes every day and he has begun to watch for her, for the silhouette of her hip as she moves away from the light, for the womanly undulation. She picks her way through the chaos and stands with her basket across the cluttered bench from him. "What now?"

"Knots. The sailors have been showing me how to tie knots. I was thinking about the kites again. So many ways to secure a simple piece of twine. Here."

"What?"

"Give me your hand."

She reaches across the bench and he takes her by the wrist.

"This, for instance is a good knot. The harder you pull the tighter it becomes. See."

He secures her wrist with a piece of cord. He looks her in the eye as he lashes the free end around the heavy vice which is bolted to the bench. She is sprawled forward across the clutter, half laughing, half frightened, unable to move, trying to undo the knot with her free hand.

"So, Naucrate, fisherman's wife of this town, caught so simply. I, Daedalus the Athenian, claim your person by right of capture."

He walks around behind her, takes the hems of her heavy skirts and throws them up over her hips. He is rapt, mesmerised by the splendour of her nakedness. She is making a sound which is neither sobbing nor laughter. He places the palms of his hands between her thighs and parts them a little. She has stopped moving. Her cleft is not quite wet. He puts saliva from his mouth on the ends of his fingers, places them inside her cunt, drawing them lightly from front to back. With a little dying movement she sinks into the bench, open to him now.

"Such regal buttocks, such fine and receptive thighs."

He speaks absently as if he were talking to himself, kneading and enticing her with his hands until she begins to move restlessly, and finally he enters her like a man coming home.

4

Daedalus notices how the hoof splays and sinks a little each time the bull's weight comes on to it. The bull moves magisterially into the sandy space, muscles running beneath the white blotched hide, and comes to a halt, its shadow black beneath it. The ageless, long lashed eye blinks. The gilding on the long sweep of its horns is chipped in places.

The sacred bull is familiar to him, yet he is always transfixed by its vast remote presence. It is like a world. Daedalus knows better than anyone how huge it is, he knows precisely. Long since, soon after he came, he and his tiny son, to Minos' island of cities, he made the replica of it, the enormous simulacrum in wood and leather and brass which stands in the bull leapers' hall. The white bull is older now, heavier and, according to the gossip of the bull court, grown unpredictable. He has heard it said that when there have been earth tremors it has become infected with a kind of madness so that no one dare go near.

He is preoccupied with the task for months together. There are endless measurements and drawings and models to be made. In the city's slaughterhouse he dissects and makes drawings of the carcass of a newly killed bullock. He has the skeleton kept and boiled clean by bemused slaves and he drills the bones and threads them onto a frame of bronze so that it stands as it would have in life. Minos is much taken by the spectral bullock when he visits the workshop, circling it on his crook legs, grinning. The skeleton is taken to his apartment in the palace when Daedalus has finished his work on the replica of the white bull. The head and neck of the wooden monster are made articulate so that the brass horns can be made to move to left and right, to raise and lower. A skilful operator can reproduce a variety of lifelike movements. Seen with the tail of the eye, tossing its great head, hurling a dancer high over its padded wooden back it seems to live, almost as if it had the soul of a bull. To see it move is to be caught in a dream of living flesh. There is a particular sequence which invokes a world between what is made and what is born: the bull's horns come in low and then hook upward and to the left in a curving sweep, sending the bull dancer in an oblique parabolic flight. Even Daedalus who knows all of its mundane, inanimate secrets has been assailed by a kind of confusion at the way it deceives the senses and invades the realm of life itself.

Within days of its completion there is uproar, particularly among the priests of the palace. There are those who claim it is sacrilegious, unnatural, the work of a necromancer. Palace gossip grows indignant, vicious. The bull leapers, who have watched and been engrossed during the weeks when Daedalus is fitting the complex machinery into the wood and leather carapace, and who have been delighted by the strange magic of its movement, now grow sulky and refuse to go near it. There are calls for it to be burnt, for Daedalus, the strange newcomer, to be banished. Though he remains in the shadow of Minos' protection, the spite and anger of the court makes itself felt, bearing down upon him in a hundred trivial ways. There are veiled insults. He is avoided, eyes sliding away from his glance. Even now, years later, he will occasionally catch someone making a furtive bad luck sign as he passes. He thinks about quitting the island altogether. He moves out of the palace and takes a room in the port overlooking the harbour, staying away from the controversy. He can drink in the bars unrecognised and unmolested.

On a squally evening at the end of summer when the sun has gone down amid lurid rags of cloud and the galleys jostle at their moorings, he has gone down to the harbourside to watch a troupe of itinerant puppeteers. The canvas of the painted booth cracks in the wind and the torches plunge and it is hard to catch the voices but the crowd is held, fixed by the drama of the wooden puppets, and Daedalus has the same sense of awe that is evoked in him by the movement of the wooden bull. Here is life itself, magically investing the inanimate. Some sticks of wood, paint, canvas, are kindled into fevered reality. Wooden arms lift, heads turn, painted eyes flash. The crowd is held, bound within the story. Afterwards, he wanders the waterfront until he finds the bar where the puppeteers are drinking. They are Egyptians, wary and suspicious, affecting not to understand him, reluctant to talk, but he buys them drinks and so they are finally obliged, under the inescapable, reciprocal law of the gift, to respond to him. As the evening wears on they become more expansive, though less intelligible as their Egyptian accents thicken in drink, recognising in some unreachable fashion that Daedalus is of their tribe, the tribe of counterfeiters. The Egyptians are people of the same extended family, more or less, fugitives years ago from some pogrom which has swept the plains of the great delta. They had been funeral puppeteers, an arcane but respectable caste in Egypt. They had acted out the soul's journey at the funerals of the rich, using masks and stately puppets almost as tall as a man. There was music and chanting. The forms of words have come down to them through the generations of their caste. The woman sitting by Daedalus begins to sing, a kind of low keening, and the men join in with wavering descants. The noise of voices in the bar ebbs to silence as the words of the funeral dirge come and go, wandering like skeins of weed in the current of a stream.

In exile they have adapted their trade to suit their outcast condition. They have made new puppets with which to act out universal stories of deception and mischief in the villages along the coast and in the mountains. The hawk faced woman who has taken up the funeral dirge speaks in her opaque accent.

"You have to be careful. The villagers are, how would you say, simple... not quick... you understand. One time, Amon here, he had his puppet snatched out of his hand in the middle of the show. In our shows it is Amon's puppet who is always the mischief maker. It was thrown onto a fire. The man who did it, who threw the puppet on the fire, he said, I got rid of him for you. He's a bad one, that one, always making mischief, spoiling your show. You're better off without him."

"It's not so funny," puts in the lugubrious Amon, "He was not so stupid, that villager. There is a soul in the puppet. That man, he knew."

The cow is tethered a few yards away but the bull does not move.

She is restless, fidgeting on the tether like a boat moored in a rising tide. Pasiphae the queen is waiting. She gives off a tense expectancy like an odour. Daedalus is standing behind her, half lost in his reverie.

These days, he keeps away from the bull leapers' hall and the teams of acrobats and dancers for whom the wooden bull is a fact of daily life, a tool of their trade, like an anvil or an oar. They are young. It was made before their time and they remember nothing else. The image of the wooden monster standing blackly against the tall windows of the practice hall while the oiled bodies fly, is a touchstone, a landmark in the country of his dreams. The horns go in low, hook upward and to the left. They seem so frail, so impossibly slight, these half grown bull leapers, a spiteful and gossipy crowd in any case. Even the boys affect a kind of sulky effeminacy so that they are barely to be distinguished from the breastless girls in the teams. On festival days, when they perform for the crowds, the bodies of the girls are painted white. You need the paint, Daedalus thinks, to know the difference. His mind drifts for a moment to the splendours of the fisherman's wife, who needs no white paint.

Of necessity, he goes to the practise hall to check or repair the bull. The dancers gather round as he removes the curved panels and reaches into its dark machinery. He is moved by their frail mortality and their childlike bickering, their bird-boned insouciance at the world's icy exit. In the packed bull court he has seen such children as these tossed about like rags. There have been accidents, even with the mechanical bull. They fall, bruise themselves, break bones. He remembers going back to file down the points of the brass horns after some bad incident. The brass itself is polished to a slick mirror surface by the grip of endless rosined hands. He does not like to think about the horns.

Something has come to the bull. The tethered cow has finally entered his consciousness. The massive head comes up, saliva looping from the muzzle. Flickering tendons run as he begins to move toward her.

During the weeks when he is setting the mechanical bull into the floor of the practise hall he has grown accustomed to the constant shouting and chatter echoing in its vaulted space. He has become familiar with the arcane gossip, the technical discussion, the small intrigues, the easy androgynous affection. They groom one another, devote hours to combing their black waistlength ringlets. Their hair is dyed with indigo so that the lights shine blue. They kiss and fondle absently, bicker like sparrows. He comes to know the lore of good luck charms and spells and the secret meanings of the gifts from half grown princesses who pant and scream in brocaded boxes high above the strange drama of the bull dance. And when one of their jewelled idols is tossed and gored to a bloody rag in the baking afternoon and the roaring mass is possessed, the little princesses are carried home cataleptic, and will take neither food nor drink and are near to death. In a month they are back in their cushioned boxes sipping the juice of persimmons mixed with crushed ice, growing breathless and wet for the oiled and bedecked flesh of a new passion.

The cow curvets distractedly on her tether. Her tail is up and her vent glistens redly. The bull's muzzle comes up against it clumsily as he fixes her with the careless force of his tongue. She shits messily in her agitation, her juices running down the smeared haunches. She is very still now, standing for him. Trembling runs across the surface of her body like the wind's catspaws. Suddenly he is on her and she staggers beneath the weight, almost losing her footing. Her legs seem to Daedalus to bend like green sticks as the bull slams home. Pasiphae sits down unceremoniously. Her throat is flushed, her mouth half open. She is lost in her own mysterious transports. Convulsions begin to ripple seismically across the bull's flesh and as he spasms the cow almost falls so that he drops back awkwardly onto his four feet, semen still jetting from the glistening red spear. The queen is clutching herself. Daedalus, ludicrously, is aware that he is trying to compute the angle at which the bull enters the cow. He too is caught up in his own flesh during these moments of rut.

When it is over, the bull keepers lead the cow away. With their long pointed goads they coax the bull circumspectly back into the dark. Beside him the queen speaks. Her voice is husky.

"What do you think? Is it possible?"

5

Naucrate is lying on her back gazing down the tawny landscape of her own body at the tiny man standing on her left kneecap. He is very small, perhaps as tall as the width of her hand. There is something hesitant about him, as if he were short sighted. He gazes myopically up towards her face and then peers all around as he stands on the little summit of her knee. Finally he sets off up the slope of her rounded thigh, his arms extended for balance. When he comes above the blond triangle of pubic hair he looks in astonishment, holding his hand to his head. Walking carefully round beneath her navel he kneels at the edge of the crinkly expanse. His hand pats it uncertainly. He rests his head on it as if contemplating sleep but gets up again and continues on his teetery way, pausing only to lower his foot gently into the hollow of her deep set navel in the way that a child will step attentively into a puddle. His foot fits the lozenge shaped space comfortably. He tries the other foot for a moment before departing. He toils up the slope of her breast and stands rapt above her large brown nipple as if he were admiring a flower, his head on one side. He kneels again and rests his cheek against the puckering dome of the teat. He sighs, lifting his shoulders hugely and letting them go before lying down with his head pillowed against the teat and his knees drawn up.

"Sssssh,' says Daedalus, folding the strings of the puppet down over the tiny stick limbs of the wooden man like a coverlet, "he's asleep'.

"You're mad,' Naucrate laughs.

He is sitting beside her on the empty floor of a derelict loft high above the workshop. There is a great square opening which looks out over the sea. Once this loft was a warehouse and a ruined hoist hangs outside over the opening, like a gallows, skeletal against the reddening sky. The wide planks of the wooden floor are littered with the debris of their passion, blankets and pillows, vases of flowers, some long dead, fruit rinds, empty bottles. They do not speak of the wistfulness which gathers in this place as the weeks pass, like the ash of memory left behind after each conflagration of the blood. They have taken to coming up the long flights of ancient wooden ladders to this eyrie after the queen's messenger stumbled upon them naked and spread-eagled between the benches of the workshop below.

Daedalus is gazing out now to the horizon where the sun is dying among lurid rags of cloud. The surface of the sea is dimming from purple to black as the day sinks toward night. Gulls turn in the melancholy light.

"I think we are all as mad as we have the liberty to be. Slaves are very sane, for example. I am a little mad myself, having a little space to be mad in. Minos, on the other hand, is as mad as he chooses to be because there is no one to gainsay him. He cannot help but be mad. His authority over others makes him so. I have never met anyone who has resisted the madness that comes with power. I could tell you a story, if you like, about madness."

"Wait a minute."

She begins to get up.

"Watch out, don't wake him."

Naucrate rolls her eyes as she lifts the little bundle of sticks gently from her breast and puts it down beside her. She pours wine into their empty glasses and settles back against him. The touch of her body brings him as close to peace as it is in his nature to be.

"Right. Go on."

"You've seen Glaucus the boy prince, Minos' son? He sometimes passes through Iraklion with a showy retinue. Well, he isn't the king's son at all. That's something else that you could be killed for knowing. That's the end of the story really. I'll start at the beginning.

One of the people I met when I came to this island was a man called Polyeidus. He was a Greek, a diplomat from the court at Mycenae. I didn't exactly meet him. I found him behind a wall. It was when I was trying to make a map of the maze of passageways and cellars under the palace. I was creeping along one of the lower levels under the megaron with my lamp, unwinding my ball of string as I went. It was an empty stretch of passageway, just rubble and rats' eyes in the lamplight and a close silence. But then I heard a sound, the moaning of a voice. At first I thought it was just some quirk, a distant voice amplified by the tunnel, but when I held my lamp aloft I could see that the masonry of the wall had been mortared recently. It looked like a walled up door and the sound seemed to come from behind it. I took a stone from the floor and banged a nail into the mortar to tie the string to, so that I could retrace my steps. It had come into my head that I would return with a chisel and a crowbar. As I started to feel my way back along the string the wall banged back.

By the time I reached the workshop I was in two minds. None of my business who gets walled up by whom, and me a newcomer to the palace, I thought. But there's no arguing with these things. You do what you do. I went back with the tools.

When I levered away the first stone, a smell of shit and rot flowed out. I thought I'd found a sewer. But it was Polyeidus. I should have recognised him because I'd caught a glimpse of him a week or two before, but I didn't. He was just a starved and stinking lunatic jabbering at me through the hole I'd made. There was a child in there too, a baby, but it was dead. It was then that I realised who he was. I had to go back for food and water. I wasn't going to let him out until I'd had the chance to think. I could hear him screaming and raving at me as I crept away for the food. By the time I got back he'd pulled away more stone and was half way to getting out. His fingers were bloodied and he was scrabbling and sobbing. I had to threaten him with the crowbar to get him to be still. "Eat and drink and then tell me your tale," I said, "and then maybe I'll let you out." I knew a part of his story already but I didn't tell him what I knew. He ate and drank like an animal and then he was sick. He was quieter after that.

I didn't get all the details of his story at the first telling. I had to make him keep going back over it. At the end of it all I couldn't tell whether he was mad or not. His name was Polyeidus. I said that. He'd been at the court a few weeks. He'd come from the court at Mycenae where it had been all boorishness and shouting generals at the palace there. He was a bit of a lout himself, with a broad back and a big jaw, though when I saw him peering out of his hole he was filthy and hollow eyed, not like a Greek hero at all. He was out of his depth amid the barbed gossip and slippery wit of the court at Cnossus, though he approved of the cut of the womens' dresses and I imagine that their eyes were caught by his big shoulders and his red hair. I expect they were curious to know what he kept under his kilt. From what he said it seems that some of them found out, though he seemed a bit alarmed in a provincial sort of way at some of the things he'd been asked to do. He thought the men small and effeminate and he punched the first one who propositioned him.

Glaucus was a baby at the time, a year old maybe, just able to walk, the apple of Minos' eye. The king used to bring him into the throne room and sit him on his knee while he condemned wretches to death. The king would pretend to consult the child as if he were a juryman, though Minos is a man addicted to killing and all condemned supplicants died anyway.

One day the boy disappeared. The palace was in uproar. Even I heard about it. Everyone except Polyeidus guessed that the baby had been killed as an act of revenge and the courtiers breathed very shallowly, knowing that Minos would find a scapegoat. He convened the court. He didn't mention his lost son at all. He told them that a heifer calf had been born on one of the mountain farms and that this heifer changed colour each day. In the morning it was white but as each day passed its colour would change to red and then to black. Minos had the doors locked. "You must all think up a simile to describe this portentous birth, an apt comparison," he told the assembled courtiers. "I shall give a prize for the best." He turned over an hourglass and the sand began to run. When the time came for these similes to be spoken out loud they all proved to be lame or ludicrous or stupid. No one in the court intended to win Minos' prize, whatever it might prove to be, except Polyeidus, who could not see the wood for the trees. He was very pleased with himself. "The heifer," he said, when it was his turn to speak, "is like nothing so much as a ripening blackberry. It is white when it first appears on the bush and turns through red to black as it ripens." The court applauded in pure rapture. Minos spoke. "The priests of the temple of the Scorpion God have told me that he who thinks up the best simile is he who will find my lost child. That is your prize, Polyeidus the Argive, the privilege of finding my son."

The Greek was banjaxed. He had thought the Cretan court a soft effeminate place and suddenly he was pinned beneath its claw. His case was desperate. The price of failure was hardly to be contemplated. Polyeidus had been at the court long enough to know something of Minos' reputation for unpredictability and sudden anger. He trailed about the palace, naively half hoping that the priests were right and that he had some gift of divination of which he himself was unaware, and got lost repeatedly. On one of these futile expeditions, when he had all but abandoned hope, a voice spoke to him out of a darkened doorway. The voice made him an offer. Polyeidus should bring a sum of money to this same spot at an arranged time and in return would be guided to the place where the child was. The sum of money specified was very large. The Greek's first impulse was to throttle the information out of his tormentor. He blundered into the darkness of the doorway and was clubbed down.

In the end he had no choice and at last he found himself standing alone, a poorer man, in a remote corner of the palace wine cellars, facing a row of big bellied wine jars almost as tall as himself, his hooded guide having slipped away into the darkness. He found an old crate to stand on. The baby was in the third jar he opened. The corpse was upside down, the wrinkled soles of its feet floating level with the surface of the wine. The little cadaver had been dyed to the colour of raw meat by the red wine in the jar.

I know that the next bit of the story he told me is true because I was there by chance in the yard above the cellars when the dead child was brought up. Minos was holding the little crimson corpse against his body. Ash had been poured over his head and shoulders and you could see the path of his tears through the grey dust on his face. He was pacing about crablike on his wasted legs with the little body in his arms, wailing like a hired mourner. Onlookers were careful to avoid his gaze. The Greek stood gawping, blank as an ox, and at last he fell under Minos' eye. The king sidled up to him, catching his brawny arm in his claw. "Speak, noble Argive. How was this achieved, this miracle?"

And then something very strange happened. Polyeidus' eyes rolled back in his head and he began to speak with the voice of the oracle. "I hear the speech of bees," he intoned, "the voice of the swarm. I am the swarming of the bees in owl light. I am the bee's wing in the eye of the owl. I am the eye of the night, the seeker in darkness."

Something like that. He stood there with his eyes rolled back and foam at the corners of his mouth. At the time it seemed a strange thing but no more than you might see at a temple ritual or in the sacrificial grove. I didn't know then that he had simply paid money and been guided to the place where the corpse was.

"This man," declaimed Minos in a broken voice between sobs, circling the entranced Greek, "this stranger has the gift. I believe he has been sent to us for a purpose. He has the gift of divination. This blessed stranger has found my child, and I have faith in him. I have faith in his gift. I believe that this man, who has restored the body of this dear infant to me can restore its life also." Minos presses the dyed corpse into Polyeidus' arms. "Take this child and restore him to life. I command it." The king gimps over to one of his bodyguards and unsheathes the man's sword. There is a universal flinching in that courtyard as the blade comes free. "Take this sword, noble Argive," he says, pressing the weapon on the Greek so that he stands like some emperor of misrule with the red corpse under one arm and the sword upright in his other hand and his face a mask of lunatic vacancy. "Take this sword. May it serve you well on your perilous journey into Tartarus to retrieve the life of my child." Minos gestures to the guard. "Take this man away. He shall have neither food nor drink until my child is restored to me."

"Are you making this up? Are you teasing me?"

Naucrate sits up and gives Daedalus a hard look.

"Do you want to hear this story or don't you? Pour me some more wine."

"Yes. I mean no. Go on."

She pours out the last of the wine.

"So, there I was, crouching in the darkness with my lamp going out, in a subterranean passageway with rats creeping over my feet, listening to a madman through a hole in a wall. The cat was out of the bag and I didn't know how to get it back in. What was I supposed to do? He wasn't going to let me brick him up again. I thought about beckoning him to put his head out through the hole in the wall and braining him with my crowbar, and then filling in the hole again. Have you ever wished you could go back, even just a few hours and live the last bit of your life again, make it come out differently? Pass the mortared up wall without a glance, better still, never have gone down into that labyrinth at all. Well, I'll tell you, I'll tell you what I did. I don't know why but this is what I did. I became a player in the mad game myself. I said, "Listen, I can get you out. I can untangle this, but you have to believe me. You have to stay here. You have to stay here and not go mad. You have to wait. Do you understand? You have to wait until I come back." And all the time I was speaking I hadn't a clue what it was that I was going to do to get him out, but he nodded. He nodded and nodded so that I was convinced he was mad. But he was nodding and that must have meant he agreed. Is that what it means, when a madman nods?

I left him and went away out of that place and I did the following things as if it had all been written down for me like a shopping list. I went to the souk and bought opium. I went to the street of the dyers and bought crimson dye. I went down to the harbour, to the office of one of the slave traders and I said to the fat Egyptian clerk after I had woken him, "I need a baby, a boy, this big. Don't take it from its mother. Find me an orphan. A year old, more or less. Black hair."

"You may be lucky," said the Egyptian, smiling his sleepy, thick lipped smile. "Ships came in yesterday. There were deaths among the saleable goods. These things are unavoidable. There may be orphans, if they haven't been disposed of. There isn't much of a market in babies, you understand. The Phoenicians sacrifice them, they say. Barbarous, barbarous. The warehouse is round the back.

You may find what you want."

The place was a reeking abattoir, a charnel house. There were corpses laid out inside the door, awaiting disposal. Gangrel gaolers, lounging. I cannot tell you. The inmost hall of hell. I didn't want to be there at all. Who wants to know, who wants to breathe the air in which these things happen? I am not a man who holds with such traffic, yet I was here. The packed iron cages stretched the length of the place. They were Thracians, whole villages in chains: men, women, children. I stood in the space between two cages and spoke to them in Greek. I explained that I wanted a baby, a boy, and that the child was to go to a rich family whose baby had died. There was a shuffling and a whisper of muttering but no one spoke. "This is a bad place full of dirt and disease. The babies in these cages will die soon anyway," I told them. "This is a chance for one of them." I looked from face to averted face. A woman met my eye, summoning me with a look. She was tall, hawklike, perhaps sixty years old, with a wild and knotted mane of grey hair.

"There is a child. Two cages that way. His father was killed when they came from the ships to burn the village. His mother died on the ship. Many died on the ship. The woman who is looking after him is not his mother. Tell her you spoke to Oenone." As I made to move away the old woman caught my arm through the bars. "Tell me," she said, "who could have made a world like this one, except a lunatic?"

I fed the baby drugged milk and dyed its ailing body crimson while it slept and carried it down to the underworld. I worked more stones loose from the wall of Polyeidus' tomb so that I could pass the sleeping infant through to him and he could pass the dead Glaucus out. The corpse stank. The Greek had eaten most of one of its arms. Ohere is nothing of which men are capable that they will not finally do. I passed through to him food and water and milk for the baby. "Wait, be patient, let the baby cry when it wakes. It will drive you mad, but let it cry." He wept as I rebuilt the wall with the new mortar I had fetched for the purpose, sealing him in darkness.

The third deputy chamberlain, a man I came to know later in different circumstances, whose name is Dassis, has an office that is like the bottom of a well, lit only by a single skylight, high up. The post of third deputy chamberlain involves a responsibility for the maintenance of the palace fabric, for bricks and mortar. Nothing is built or repaired in the palace that he does not know about. "Forgive me for disturbing you," I said from within the folds of my disguise, "but I have heard a baby cry. In the tunnels beneath the megaron." As I left his office he was holding on to the edge of his table with both hands. That's it."

"What do you mean, that's it?"

Naucrate sits up, spilling the lees from her glass over her thigh.

"Well, it worked. Dassis sent men down to the place in the tunnel and they heard the baby cry. Minos was summoned and a torchlit procession of courtiers and masons and hangers on made their way down though the winding passageways and stairs. I seemed to understand Minos' madness and I foresaw how it would be in that underground theatre. Minos' madness is the madness of an actor who cannot quit his part in the drama. The audience stood in a hushed semicircle as the masons broke down the wall. The king takes a torch and steps inside and there in the flickering light is Polyeidus holding his sword in one hand and the baby in the crook of his other arm, newly returned from the dark fields of asphodel. Minos puts his fingers to the sleeping infant's neck and feels the slight patter of the blood beneath the skin. The moment cannot be denied. The actor king must play out his part."

"But someone must have guessed." Naucrate objects, her brow furrowed in consternation. "One of his nurses, his mother, the king. When they got him up into the light, when he was bathed and examined. How could they not know?"

"Death changes us. The child was ill when I took it from the Thracian woman. He came near to death and the drama of his return to life gripped the palace and the city. Who could have said, this is not the child? This is not Glaucus, the prince. Who, even suspecting, would have been so foolish? Even Minos himself was trapped in his own fiction.

Something else too. When Minos spoke to the Greek, the big man was possessed by his fit again. He told a garbled tale of snakes bearing holy herbs in their mouths. He told how he killed a snake in that room in the underworld and how he watched its mate bring herbs in its mouth and restore the dead snake to life. The Greek described how he took the herbs and applied them to the body of the infant prince and he began to breathe again."

"You made this story up. I know you did."

"Shall I tell you something else? It was Minos who had put his child to death in the first place."

"You are mad. You're mad if the story's true and you're mad if you made it up."

"I'll tell you one more thing. When Polyeidus sought permission to leave the court and return to Mycenae about three or four years later, Minos told him that before he would allow him to leave he must teach Glaucus the secret art of divination which had allowed him to find the prince and restore him to life. The Greek spent hours with the little boy, teaching him this mystery. When the day of his departure came the boy accompanied him to the harbour with his nurse to wave him off. Polyeidus kissed the boy and whispered to him, "When I open my mouth, spit into it." He opened his mouth and the child spat into it and in that moment he forgot all that the Greek had taught him."

"You are mad, definitely. How do you think these things up? I'm late. I have to go."

She sweeps up her clothes. He can hear her descending the long ladders below. Outside, the gibbet outline of the ruined hoist is silhouetted against the last streaks of the dying sun. Beside him on the floor, the tiny man moves in his sleep as if his dreams were bad.

6

In Gournia town below the hilltop sprawl of the palace and the temple there is a market. It is a big market, spreading out from the town square along the streets which radiate from it, with booths and stalls on both sides of the road. These streets are solid with people. The market square itself is a world of fruit and vegetables and flowers. The farmers who have come in through the night from outlying farms with their strings of laden mules lay out their produce in opulent mounds and patterns on the flagstones. There is much pouring of water through the hot day to keep things fresh. In the narrow shadowed streets of the town everything that can be thought of is for sale. The street of the dyers stuns the eye, a forest of brilliantly coloured bolts of cloth hanging in looped and festooned confusion overhead, yellow, purple, indigo. In the coloured shadows beneath, crowds move. Where the rope vendors have their stalls the air is thick with the dark reek of flax.

The pottery of Gournia is known throughout the islands and dealers come from all parts of the archipelago. Between the stacked crates of tiles an Egyptian merchant hunkers down to barter, his hands eloquent, a world of offended disbelief in the raising of a hennaed palm. There are whole districts of bowls, amphorae and oil jars, lamps, cups and piled shelves of statuettes. The sound of clay whistles carries over the market din. These whistles are in the shape of birds and when you fill them with water and play, they make a warbling sound like a nightingale. The vendor of clay bulls and statuettes of the snake mother is shaking the straw from his wares and setting them out on the shelves of his stall. He is late, still drunk, and the day is half over. A few feet away the Anatolian vendor of glass beads is burning a dried chameleon in a bowl of charcoal, blinking in the smoke.

"My eyes are bad. The smoke of the chameleon is a sovereign cure for disorders of the eye," he informs the vendor of bulls politely.

The vendor of clay bulls wonders whether the smoke of the chameleon might work for a bad head and a queasy belly.

There is a space between mean mud houses which is devoted to the trade in goats. You can find it by following the smell. Along the road running out of the town to the south, horse dealers tether the mares with their foals. Naked babies play under the hooves. There are painted carts and chariots upended in rows.

As the day fades into a bleached out mid afternoon the crowds thin and there is a drifting away, a repacking of dusty wares, a gathering lassitude. It is the end of summer and the fruit in the market is overripe. Wasps darken the air and feed where the skin splits. Underfoot the ground is sticky. Sudden quarrels break out. An enraged carter takes his whip to a woman in the crowd. There is a sullen surging, angry shouting rises above the noise of the street.

Above the emptying town, the late afternoon grows overcast and still. The dark is coming on early. The mountains are silent. There seems to be no movement in all the miles of air. No bird drifts in the void. The sky hangs like a curtain in a temple. The stillness is vast, empty, expectant. But now there is something imagined, a slow falling, an invisible downward motion which is everywhere. It is as if the whole sky were beginning to fall, slowly and invisibly. It is ash. Through this falling of ash comes another falling, a falling through the falling, a heavier faster rain of visible particles. The sky darkens to a universal grey descending.

The vendor of clay bulls is giving up for the day: he is still not himself. He will stay out of the brothel tonight, he tells himself as he begins to wrap up the unsold pieces in straw rope and repack them. Only hoofprints in the day's dust remain on the wooden shelves. He runs his finger through the unfamiliar dust. It is thick and bitter on the tongue. Up the street it hangs like fog. Figures move like shades in an underworld of grey. A slow dry rain is falling, the ashy unslaking rain which falls in dreams. There is a looking up, a helpless exchanging of glances. There is no name for what is happening. The fog of ash thickens. Close by he can hear the voice of the bead seller praying. The vendor of clay bulls is alone beneath the grey bitter sea. There is a sound of thunder and the slow rain of ash turns to a killing deluge of stones. He creeps beneath the roaring boards of his stall. Bulls dance into shattered oblivion.

7

Bare arsed, the queen is sitting in a large, four-legged wicker basket. Daedalus has a doubtful look on his face as he contemplates her.

"It won't work like that. If the bull thrusts too hard he'll break your legs. You'll have to kneel, on all fours. That way you can move forward if you need to, and in any case it will be easier that way to guide him in with your hand. You can reach between your legs."

He holds out his hand and she steps out of the contraption to the platform which stands beside it. Pasiphae's rounded belly and the deep set navel are level with his head, the blue black thatch of hair and the tattooed snakes coiling round her thighs. Daedalus knows that only dead men see these things. This is Pasiphae, the god king's bride, priestess of the snake mother, the very embodiment of what is forbidden. She bends, sweeping up her heavy hooped skirt and descends to the floor. He says,

"There is no way I can make it safe, or even be sure it will work. The bull may not even come to you."

"Oh, it will come to me, my magician, because I desire it. You desire it too, I know you do."

She pulls apart the knot on his belt, reaching down inside his tunic, grasping him with both hands. Her eyes widen in mock surprise.

"You see, so hard. A fine thing you have down here, but I must have the bull, my magician, I am Io the Moon Cow and I must have the bull."

"Is not Minos the bull ? The queen is the cow and the king the bull. That is what people say."

She turns on him, hissing, venomous.

"You speak like a man who wants to die. Minos is a cripple, a deformity. When he comes to his crooked climax he spills out serpents and scorpions. He has no taste for this."

She runs her outstretched hand down her belly and deep between her thighs and holds up her glistening fingers in a fierce gesture that is like an angry benediction. She stands blazing like a fire, arm outstretched toward him, burning in her rage. The moment ebbs, becomes the past. With a gentle deft movement she strokes the wetness from her fingers across his hollow cheeks, anointing him.

"No, Minos has none of your appetite, magician, none of your weakness. He can hear only where there is speech. He cannot hear the dark voice of the act itself. He does not know, will never know."

Naked, with her clothes over her arm, she walks out to her women who are waiting beyond the jagged hole in the wall that will never be a door.

8

The fisherman's wife enters hesitantly through the jagged doorway. She does not see him at first in the half dark as he stitches the leather to the wicker cow's vent. Not a job for a sane man, he thinks. Still, it is beginning to look something like a cow's arse. He has become an expert in these things, hanging around the slaughterhouse, drawing the backsides of cows, while the slaughtermen exchange glances. Do bulls have particular tastes, he wonders, do they even notice the variety of their concubines?

She is standing behind him and he has not noticed. He jumps when she speaks, sticking the sewing needle into his finger.

"I have come because I am hot. Feel how hot I am."

She takes his hand and lifts her skirt. She is wet already and he is instantly lost. He has her abruptly against the crumbling wall, still dressed, pulling down her blouse to free her breasts. She comes noisily, he comes, and they remain standing, panting and sweating, spent.

"You shouldn't be here, not in here, its not safe."

"Why? Because of this?"

She slips beneath his arm and walks over to the wicker cow, smoothing her skirts down as she goes. Though there is no top to it yet she knows immediately.

"It's for the queen. She wants the bull to possess her."

"And if she knows you know, she'll have you killed."

"I have seen her coming in here with her women, and that poor boy carrying that great parasol."

"Did you hear what I said? You should go. Don't come in here again. We'll both go. Come on. What did you bring to eat today?"

He bustles her back out into the long workshop. They open the double doors which give onto the quayside again. She rummages about on the benches inside until she finds one of the discarded kites, insisting he help her launch it. It swoops around the sky above them as they eat.

She speaks, her mouth full,

"Sometimes I think about an octopus possessing me, all those tentacles going everywhere. It's a sort of dream I have. Do you have dreams like that?"

"I don't know. I dream about your buttocks and the muscles in your calves. From now on I'll dream about you dreaming about the octopus."

"There used to be a dog. It would come into the house and it would lick me if I let it, here."

"And did you let it?"

"Sometimes. It seemed to know."

"I wish the queen had developed a passion for the chamberlain's lapdog, a goat, anything. This business with the bull is going to get me killed. If she gets hurt I'm a dead man. What if she gives birth to a monster?"

"Why are you doing it, making this thing for her?"

"Because she tells me to, and because she put her hands down my kilt."

She looks at him scandalised, unable to tell if he's joking.

"But mostly it's because she'll have me killed if I refuse."

"When I think about it, her and the bull, it excites me. Does it excite you, making this thing for her and the bull?"

"Mostly it frightens me and it gives me a headache trying to think how to do it."

"But it excites you too?"

"Yes, that too."

"It's hot out here. Don't you think it's hot? Let's go inside."

9

Three slave ships are moored by their sterns to the harbour wall, giving off darkness and the stench of depravity. Daedalus walks in and out of the deep shadows which the high stern posts cast across his path. He walks out beyond the waterfront to the steep shingle beach where the fishing boats are drawn up or nod in the offing. Nets hang in the sun and gulls jostle for fish heads in the shallows. He catches sight of his son's hair, a red blond smudge against the pitched black strakes of a boat that is drawn up under a tree, chocked and propped clear of the ground. The boat looks as if it were sitting in the tree. A bucket of pitch smokes over a pale flotsam fire. Icarus is black to the elbows, kneeling in the black blotched white sand. The skin of his broad shoulders is burnt and peeling. He works the pitch into the caulking of the boat with that childlike absorption which is grievous to watch and hard to bear for those who know the world better. Kneeling at his back Daedalus puts his arms about the young man, weeping into his hair. Icarus pauses, smiling his glad, empty smile.

"Look, I have brought you some things."

Daedalus empties the big straw bag onto the sand.

"A shirt, a blue one, you need a new shirt. I bought it in the market."

He holds up the shirt against the boy's chest and Icarus beams and nods.

"And look, a cheese and some pomegranates and some money, and this, I brought you this too. Come."

Daedalus picks up the kite and the ball of twine, walks away from the beach and up on to the white promontory of rock above. Icarus is a head taller than his father and broader in the shoulder. Daedalus shows him how to launch the kite. It rises boisterously in the breeze. The boy is rapt as he lets it out, plunging and rising. Daedalus sits and watches for half an hour and still his son is intent on the swooping kite and will not come away.

Sinon, the boat's owner is down by the nets, a slight, dark man whose left leg is wasted. He nods affably as Daedalus trudges along the shingle toward him. He takes the fisherman's hand.

"He looks well. The life suits him. You have been good to him."

"He is a good boy, though not over talkative."

There is half a smile in his voice. Icarus has never spoken, never learned to speak.

"He seems in good spirits."

"You should have seen him yesterday. My sister's boys filled him up with red wine, heavy red, no water. It was a wedding, my cousin's daughter's. Yesterday he was like a corpse."

"I am grateful to you, Sinon. At the palace they were turning him into a performing animal, teaching him tricks. He is better here, away from the court."

"As I said, he's a good boy, strong, useful. Not quick, but an easy nature. He can splice a cable as well as I do it myself."

"I have left him some money, for what he needs."

"You shouldn't bother. He earns his keep."

"I shall be gone up to Cnossus for a week or two. If I'm delayed, look after him."

Sinon gives him a look.

"Don't worry, I'll keep him safe for you."

The kite is still dancing over the promontory as Daedalus looks back from among the fishing boats. He walks away in the sea's edge, now paddling in the wavelets, now leaving footprints in the wet sand, until he is lost against the sweep of the coast and the shapes of the distant town.

10

Above the horned rooftops of Cnossus palace, the sky is overcast, grapedark. The palace is a vague shadowless dream, a roofscape of white and cerulean blue sprawling in vacancy. The hiss of court gossip hangs in the stairwells and anterooms like the echo of an echo: an eagle has been seen carrying a snake: in the mountains a woman has given birth to a toad.

Out of season, a wind begins to blow from the east, driving before it clouds of grey dust. It has a bitter taste and catches in the throat. For days together these curtains of dry grey dust billow across the long flanks of the hills and at last, beneath the dust, comes an army of the houseless dead, a host of grey penitents in ragged files and columns trudging under the ashen wind. They walk silently like ashcloth mourners through the streets of the town and come slowly to a halt in the squares and public gardens. They have no baggage, no carts or carriages or horses. They are shriven, empty of all but life. They stand or sink down, red rimmed eyes unseeing.

They have walked from Gournia, out of a country buried beneath smoking stones and deep drifting ash, a terrible dead land. They have walked for days through an unknown desert where the sun does not dispel the night but hangs in twilight at the zenith, believing that the world has ended, until at last the darkness recedes and their broken feet walk on the earth again. It is as if they have died but not been granted the rest that comes with death, have been forced back into the world of the living.

The town fills by degrees with these ghosts until every street corner is occupied and the public spaces are seas of grey faces, and still they arrive. The smell of their presence is detectable in every alleyway, a smell sulphurous, ashy. Behind half closed shutters the townspeople stand in the shadow, in fear of the contagion of death, watching the silent unending columns filing into the town. Some are brought indoors out of limbo by aged crones or pregnant wives but it is a locust swarm. So many, so many. There is a gathering of darkness in the soul of the town, a premonition of evil. Lightnings flicker along the horizon.

Daedalus has ridden off with a group of refugees in a cart down to the port. They sit, inert as sacks, as the cart jolts down to the coast. He leads them to one end of his cavernous workshop, a dark, rubble strewn space, and fetches them what blankets and small comforts he can find. They stand about as he makes a fire. A little life is kindled out of nothing: a fire, a few fish brought by the fisherman's wife, a little overripe fruit begged from the market. They have neither money nor property of any kind. They exist in the penumbra, on the edge of the shadow. They speak hardly at all, lost in the echoing passageways of recollection, where waking is a dream and dreaming a waking nightmare. In sleep they cry out.

There are other groups who have made their way down from Cnossus to the coast. They camp in the abandoned gardens and boarded up houses of rich families, departed years ago to estates in Egypt and the mainland, fleeing the fear of earthquake. These newcomers are the absolute embodiment of that fear, yet they make few demands, except upon the imagination. Those who have money hang about the harbour like newly dead souls on the banks of the Styx, waiting to take ship. They depart for who knows where. There are shadowy agreements between the captains of tradeships in the offices of the slavers and not all of the refugees reach the destinations they anticipate.

11

Daedalus sits with his hands locked across his knees in the circle around the fire. It burns whitely and is made with the bones of antique ships. Monstrous shadows leap in the vault. The small man next to him leans towards him and whispers,

"I don't suppose you have a dead chameleon about you, sir? The smoke of a burning chameleon is a sovereign cure for disorders of the eye, and my eyes are bad, sir, indeed I can barely see. I fear I am going blind. Though I will be frank, I have no money, not even my bags of beads to pay you with. I lost them in that town. They were buried under the ash and stones."

He falls silent again. Daedalus is close to tears, but does not know the reason. The voice begins again.

"Wherever I travel I have always found the trade in glass beads to be reliable. There is that in a bead which attracts the eye to look and the hand to pick up. Anatolian beads are much sought after by those who know about such things. There have been bead makers in my family for as long as anyone can remember. My first memory, I think, is of the shape of my father's head against the light of his bead furnace. I am the youngest of seven and so there was no place for me in the business of making beads. A bead furnace is a remarkable thing, like a little domed house whose windows are lit with a fierce light. The molten beads glow like tiny suns.

I became a seller of beads, a packman, around the towns and villages of my native country. You see, beads are costly in relation to their weight. A donkey can carry enough beads to sustain a season's trade. I found the life suited me well. I talk easily to strangers. I like to see the country.

As the seasons passed, I began to go further and further afield. I arranged to have consignments of beads sent to reliable souks so that I no longer needed to return home. Travel became my life and, if you will pardon the expression, my passion. I walked my donkey eastward for four years along the routes the camel trains take and I may tell you sir that the world is a bigger place than it is possible to know. When you have seen so many cities, so many mountains, deserts and broken stony places it is no longer possible to think of your own life as of any importance at all. There is a comfort in this, I think. I saw many strange and remarkable things on my travels. I was robbed, more than once, and have brushed close to death. I am a small man who travels alone. Robbers must think me an easy target.

I came home again. I had used up several donkeys, some of them noble beasts. But you know, a donkey's constitution is frailer than that of a man. When a donkey has come to the end he knows. He will put his head down and die. It is not so with a man. A man lives as if there were no end.

My family did not seem to be quite so pleased to see me as I had hoped and my little nieces and nephews did not know me at all. And so, after a few weeks, I arranged to have beads sent as far West as I prudently could and I set off again. Do you know Egypt at all? I had a shop in the bazaar close to the great temple in Karnak for some years and business was good. I had friends and a house, but I missed the travel. Staying in one place for so long began to weigh upon me. I am no longer a young man, as you may see, but there is a restlessness in me which the years do not diminish and which refuses all argument. I sold my house and furniture and my shop by the temple and bought a donkey. And that is how I came to be in Gournia town."

The old man pauses again and Daedalus knows that behind the closed eyes the waves of memory are breaking over him. He is sitting cross legged in front of a dying fire, abiding, an unmoving stone beneath the tide. After a little while he opens his eyes.

"Gournia had a good market. People have an eye for what is well made or unusual. I had been there a few weeks. I had a stall next to a vendor of statuettes of the snake mother. He made little clay bulls too and his work was very fine, delicate, you know, possessed of life almost, but a drinker I fear, and a frequenter of whorehouses. Often the stall next to mine was empty until noon. He came late and his head was bad, from the drink, you understand. His hands trembled so much as he set out his wares that I feared he would break his statuettes of the snake mother. They were fine things, these statuettes, though he once told me that he exaggerated the size of the breasts to encourage sales, which seems an impious thing."

His voice falters and he turns to Daedalus, his voice unsteady.

"I think maybe he was joking. I looked at the breasts on those statuettes, often. They were ample, certainly, but then I understand that the snake mother is a goddess and a certain …plenitude, is that the word, is only proper to a goddess, don't you think?"

His brow furrows as if he were still trying to decide whether or not the vendor of clay bulls had given his figures large breasts to improve sales. Unexpectedly, his face crumples utterly and dry sobbing clenches his frame. He holds himself, rocking, until he is quiet again.

Daedalus says, "I think that he did not make the breasts a certain size to improve his trade. He made them a certain size because that is how he made them. These things do not come through thought or speech but through the hands."

"You know, you are right. It is the same with beads."

His expression wavers momentarily on the brink of grief again but he continues,

"You must forgive me, sir, I have been taking up your time. You see, I thought that if I told my tale from the beginning that I should be able to speak about what happened in that town, to take myself unawares, but I find I cannot. The vendor of clay bulls was a man. Beneath his coarseness there was delicacy. He died and I did not. Many thousands of people died and I did not. When the horror was over and I crept out from my hiding place it seemed as if the world had ended, that I was alone and lost in a piled and smoking desolation of blackened stones. Just in front of the hole I crept out of, there was an arm. It stuck up out of the ash like a winter tree. I believe it belonged to a young woman. There was a ring on the finger.

I am trying but I am not quite certain that I can find my way back out of that desolation."

12

Something like a bright bird sails down the workshop. It lands at the feet of the fisherman's wife. She picks it up. It is made in the same fashion as a kite but its shape is more birdlike, while beneath it hangs a small clay replica of a man in a harness made from knotted string. Daedalus comes running after it.

"See, no ball of twine. It flies. Some things have come to me. Ideas, solutions, like birds in the night."

He takes the basket of food and the kite from her.

"Come, I have been here for hours. I cannot remember when I ate last."

In the sunlit doorway behind, a movement of shadow makes them turn, a glimpse of a mirrored parasol, dark veiled women. Pasiphae steps through the door unaccompanied. The fisherman's wife grips Daedalus' arm. Unused to the gloom the queen stands uncertainly for a moment until she makes out Daedalus and his companion.

"Ah, magician, I had hoped to find you here. It came to me in the night that time is pressing. The moon is already past the full. A full moon is propitious. The moon of the equinox is full in nineteen days from now. Nineteen days is right, I think. Some things are better achieved under a full moon, don't you think?"

Her question falls on the fisherman's wife. There is a meeting of eyes, a complicity, a rising up. Daedalus says,

"This is Naucrate, a woman of this town and a friend of mine."

"A friend of yours? I am glad to meet you, Naucrate."

Pasiphae takes her hand and holds it amiably, turning it in her own.

"She is a beautiful woman, magician, and a married one I think."

She cocks an eyebrow at the fisherman's wife who returns her gaze with half a smile. Daedalus is aware that much is passing that he cannot follow.

"But then I am a married woman myself."

Pasiphae laughs, frank, complacent. She takes Naucrate by the arm.

"The magician is making something for me and I shall have need of it soon."

She turns, her eye on Daedalus, black, steely.

"Before the month is out, you must bring what you have made to the palace, or I shall grow vexed. You would not like it at all if I grew vexed."

13

It is perfectly dark. He stands behind the heavy drapes with the queen's ring in his hand. He is being pushed from behind. A woman's voice is sibilant. Go, go, she is waiting. He gropes blindly forward through the curtain.

The queen's chamber is a dim confusion of glint and flicker. Candle flames dance in a hundred lacquered surfaces. An expanse of polished floor is darkly alive with the glow of reflected lamplight. The smell in the chamber is heavy, cedar smoke, incense, flesh. She is there, Io the moon cow, on all fours. Her long nippled breasts hang, her oiled belly is deep. Coiled serpents glint blue black around her thighs. Her hair falls forward so that her face is obscured. He kneels behind her and parts her buttocks, pushing his tongue wetly into the cleft. It comes to him as he curls over her back and enters her, wasplike, that he is where the bull will be. In the cosmic tree there are two birds. One eats and the other watches it eat. He couples with the queen and he watches that coupling as from a distance. He comes with a jolt and she falls forward onto her elbows with a cry.

She curls like an infant in the womb. He pushes back the hair from her face. Great tears well from beneath the closed eyelids. She speaks out of her darkness.

"See me, magician. I am Pasiphae the queen, snake mother, Itone, rainmaker, and I am afraid and tearful. The story of my body and my passion is already written in the blood, acted out, gone down long ago. My acts are the speech of women, their history, but oh, magician, I am afraid. Let this cup pass from me. Help me to bear what I cannot bear."

14

Each morning the temples are full of people and the smoke of sacrifice rises over the rooftops of the port. Wild men are preaching the last days on rocky outcrops above the town and priests skulk, fearing retribution.

Day by day news arrives with incoming ships. Staring mariners avidly tell and tell again what they have seen to the crowds gathered along the wharf. They tell of sailing for days through scum and dead fish and strange sea creatures of monstrous size. The island of Thera has gone. What remains of its cities and its fertile slopes is a sulphurous and foggy lake of boiling seawater. Towering cliffs of red ash rise out of the sea in a broken circle, marking the edge of the crater. Steam and smoke passes upward through the clouds in a vast column. Of the cities on that island and their peoples, nothing remains. Islands to the south and east are featureless deserts of ash. The whole eastern end of Crete itself is an empty, unfamiliar wasteland. Gilded temples on the Nile, a thousand miles away, are filmed with grey.

Overcrowded ships appear out of the cataclysm like vessels from Tartarus. It is hard to know if the grey faces that line the rails belong to the living or the dead. Many of these ships leave again, inexplicably. Earth tremors are felt in the town and there is a sound like distant thunder, faint but unceasing, as of a furnace burning in hell. Houses are boarded up and abandoned as the flight of the rich is renewed. Reality shivers like the vibrating surface of the water in the harbour.

In these apocalyptic days the sun goes down in a dream of boiling crimson and the air itself reddens, thickens to lurid darkness, shroudlike. Night falls while the copper coloured sun is still above the horizon. The townspeople take to sleeping in the streets to avoid the possibility of being buried under their own houses, so that the night time has an odd festive feeling. People who have never met before sit and talk the night away around the gloze of braziers. Away from the firelight bodies couple blindly, search out the warm still centre. In the chill dark before dawn a man's voice sings, deep and strong. The livid sunrise comes like a gift and each new day has a savour when the next is a hostage. It is a time of portents and prodigies. A ship comes out of the horizon under full sail and strikes the shore a mile from the town. All those on board are long dead, their faces swollen and blackened. The timbers and the sail of the ship, the cordage and the corpses are stained a sulphurous yellow and there is a reek of brimstone.

Daedalus spends these days at the crumbling edge of the world in a sort of exultation. At the brink of destruction what is put together or made with the hands grows luminous. The life of the made thing, of the image, is flamelike. He watches the floor of his workshop ripple and listens to the sad groaning of the world beneath his feet. Water in a bucket loops into the air and splashes noisily back. Fine dust dances in a haze from every surface. The jagged lightning crack high up in the wall widens as he watches. Loosened stones arc into the void. He bends again to what he is doing, working in that perfect space between the making and the unmaking. He works long hours through these contingent days and Naucrate comes often to the workshop. After they have done with one another he likes to watch her wander naked among the clutter, idling like a nymph in the forests of his calling.

His little troupe of pilgrims have taken to spending their days fishing from the beach. They are immune to the panics and alarms in the town. They have died already and exist in the fatal moment. The beadseller who cannot see well enough to bait the hooks exchanges the catch for other necessaries in the half empty market place. The end of the workshop where they are encamped now has an assortment of conveniences for living. There are makeshift screens and an eccentric collection of furniture contrived from the wreckage of the ancient ships which half fills this part of the huge building. The people in the ragged band are old mostly, men and women, a couple of grandchildren. They exist without complaint, making a small life amid the convulsing ruins of time.

15

The wicker cow is finished. It is an unlovely object, Daedalus thinks, braced and padded within to withstand the assault which will be made upon it. Sheeted down, he drives it in a bullock cart up the paved road to Cnossus. It is a slow journey. He passes slave gangs toiling to fill in the riven and fissured surface of the highway. He has to wait an hour until they fill in a deep crevasse which has opened up across the road, with baskets of stones. High above the shiplike swaying of the bullock team he sits immobile through the hours as the cart grinds noisily upward, his mind a shutter banging in a gale of possibilities. His thinking has the materiality of the stuff of the world itself: mass, motion, force. The bull is the centre of his private vortex. It moves like a fortress of blood and sinew through his thinking dreams. He feels its weight bearing down upon the queen's fluid, insubstantial body curled within the wicker egg, a great hammer of bone which could as well burst her peach flesh as drive home into her womb the glistening sword of potentiality.

Along the approach to Cnossus town packs of dogs roam in the twilight over newly dug earth. The town itself seems silent. The faces he sees in doorways are hooded, masklike. The heavy wheels roll noisily to a stop on the crushed grit of a palace courtyard. He sits for a moment, aware of the ludicrously suggestive covered shape behind him, guessing at eyes behind blinds. He groans inwardly, knowing that events have rucked too thick for his extrication. He knows that the queen's passion will be an open secret in the court.

He goes to speak to Pasiphae. He wants a team of bull leapers in attendance to draw off the bull in case of mishap, but she will have none of it. She will not agree to anyone being present save her women and himself. He tells her it is madness. She agrees, catching his eye, mocking him.

There is an old bull court in the many layered warren of the palace, a crypt like place, abandoned for generations, a place built over and rebuilt over, known to few. Daedalus found it years ago during his attempts to make a map of the palace's brainlike pathways. The floors of the corridors and anterooms of the palace which lie above this forgotten hall sound hollowly under the footfall. He stands twenty feet below bright, sumptuous rooms in which jewelled courtiers gossip and move about, in this mouldering space, with a lamp whose light does not penetrate its farthest reaches. The low vault of the ceiling is cracked, its symmetry weirdly adrift. The coursed masonry undulates like ancient rock strata. Rotted doorframes sag into the darkness of smaller vaults which give off the oval space. It is a tomblike place, acrid with the smell of centuries. Daedalus is oblivious to these things. It will do, this place. He explores the lesser vaults in the guttering light. He needs a space to pen the white bull until the appointed time and another to pen a cow in season. He has decided that Pasiphae's powers of attraction need bolstering. It has occurred to him to smear the vent of the wicker cow with the juices of a cow's heat, though he recognises this thought as simple minded juju. Practicalities jostle in his head, though he knows that he is dreaming, making it all up like a storyteller who needs only to convince the half attentive listener, but all the time the bull is a fatal house waiting to fall on him.

He goes back to Pasiphae. "I need some help," he tells her. "I know nothing about bulls. What if there is a mishap?" She shakes her head, smiling and toying with the belt of his tunic. He explains that he must use the palace bull keepers to move the white bull into the subterranean bull court. He does not mention the cow. In the face of his consternation, she agrees. "Tell them it is a ceremony which must be performed in secret." She raises an amused eyebrow. It is as if her fear had been a dream. Her tears are not even a memory.

Daedalus takes the queen's ring with its carved seal for a second time and goes in search of the royal bull keepers. They are a strange sodality the bull keepers, large silent men, shaven headed like bulls themselves, a hereditary caste, half mad, Daedalus imagines, from generations of interbreeding. When he takes them down to the underground hall and explains what he needs they stand, grouped like cattle, sucking their teeth and shaking their heads, but the queen's ring impresses. He follows them back to their quarters where they stamp more wax tablets than seems quite necessary, applying the ring with solemn punctilio, examining the results in the wax each time, exchanging looks, nodding or pursing their lips.

He goes to the practice hall and engages the bull leapers in what he hopes is oblique conversation and comes away with a mirrored cape such as the bull leapers use and some half digested advice. He walks through the maze of passageways wondering how the huge creature can be controlled. He thinks about a tether and a winch. He thinks about a hobble, but then the bull will need to be free to mount the wicker cow. He is out of his depth. He thinks about a sledge hammer, recognising his own thought as foolishness but then nothing else comes to him. A minute later another thought bursts. Fire, he will use fire.

16

Dassis, a Persian by birth, was a deputy chamberlain when Daedalus first arrived in Cnossus years ago. It was he who paid Daedalus' wages in those days and who had helped him organise the installation of the mechanical bull. He was, is, the nearest thing to a friend. As third deputy chamberlain his chief responsibility was the maintenance of the fabric of the palace buildings. He looked after the teams of masons, the gardeners and slaves who worked for the royal house. When Daedalus had completed his first maps of the warren of deserted passageways and rooms which lay beneath the palace he took them to Dassis.

"I want to make a maze, a labyrinth. See, here, I have made a map."

He unrolls wide sheet of parchments across the chamberlain's table. There are several sheets, one for each level of the warren below the palace.

"It is a map of the tunnels and abandoned rooms under the palace. Look, I have marked out places where passageways could be blocked off, and here and here are passageways that are filled with fallen masonry which could be cleared. You would need stairs here and here. There are places that need shoring up and there are passages I can't get into yet. I could make a place of such complexity, it would be like a mind, endless, inescapable, but yet systematic, subject to a subtle law so that anyone knowing its secret could find a way through. What do you think?"

"What do I think? What do you expect me to think? I think you're mad."

"No, you don't understand. It would be an enigma, a mystery."

"I understand perfectly. Do you suppose my workteams have nothing better to do?"

Daedalus left his office, spent by the effort to speak about what was in him, and feeling like a fool, but as he went out of the door

Dassis pulled the maps toward him across the table. A few weeks later the chamberlain sent a message to say that because work in the palace was slack he may have a few masons to spare for a week or two.

Over the years since, whenever Dassis has had the men to spare Daedalus has worked on the labyrinth. The chamberlain comes with him sometimes. They have broken open ancient ways into the depths, and found tunnels of huge cyclopean stones, passageways worn smooth by unknown generations of feet. They have found clear springs of water and the entrances to natural caves which Daedalus has never yet explored. There are places where round, mancrushing stone discs rest in recesses ready to be rolled into place to block the tunnels. And everywhere the remnants of lives, the debris of existences long forgotten: bones, fragments of cloth that crumble at the touch, broken pottery, walls scrawled and inscribed with faded, inscrutable images, the ancient black stains of candle smoke on low ceilings.

And always there is more to be discovered, more to be opened up, mapped, understood, stairways to be dug out, unknown tunnels to be cleared. The labyrinth has no end. Sometimes Daedalus goes down to the lowest depths alone and blows out his lamp, kneels in that ancient and utter darkness, moving his hands blindly over stones hewn by himself a thousand years, ten thousand years ago, when he did not know who he was. He rests in what has been made, dreams its enduring anonymity. He lies flat on the cold black stones, his cheek against the marks of the claw.

Daedalus is familiar with the chamberlain's office, a small room of enormous height, like a well, lit by a solitary skylight high overhead. Daedalus finds Dassis at his table. He sits in his high ceilinged room, a haunted house of a man, the deepset, heavylidded eyes blackened as if by fatigue. His smooth skinned eunuch flesh hangs in heavy dewlaps.

"Daedalus! Welcome, welcome'

He clasps Daedalus in his arms and there is a tremor, an ague, in his flesh. His familiar voice contains something which Daedalus does not remember, something broken.

"Sit. Sit."

He sweeps a bench free of clutter.

"So busy these days, so busy, what with all the damage from the earthquakes. The palace is falling down, you know. Whole wings will need rebuilding. The tremors have opened up cracks and fissures everywhere. The great staircase is in danger of collapse and I have had it sealed off."

The chamberlain goes through a litany of his professional woes.

"My work teams are exhausted. And of course, we had to bury the dead."

Daedalus looks at him, awaiting an explanation, watching the fat man's face evolve into a mask of suffering. Dassis stares out from this mask like a prisoner.

"The good people of Cnossus town have killed the survivors who arrived from Gournia. In a single night my fellow citizens butchered these people, all of them. Nine thousand, my men buried, hewn and torn and dismembered, in pits. The world has ended, Daedalus. We are in hell."

17

The ancient paint on the ceiling of his cell-like room in the palace hangs in little volutes like wood shavings or the bark of the silver birch. He tries but cannot remember how the ceiling looked when he first arrived, how many years ago? Was it the same? He seems to remember stooping into the whitewashed cell holding on to Icarus' small hand, but that is all. These days he sleeps here seldom, preferring his workshop on the coast.

Daedalus lies on the narrow bed, sleepless, waiting, listening to the faint, distant roar of the volcano that is like the sound of blood in his veins. It is a noise which has grown so familiar that it has almost passed out of consciousness, but yet retains its power to oppress. Perhaps he does not sleep because his stomach aches and his stomach aches because he is afraid. His eyes flick to the small high window. The night is still black. He knows a full moon is riding in white splendour in the clear and endless cold beyond the cloud mantle which hangs over Cnossus. He thinks about Dassis and his mask of suffering, about the dead in their tumbled, intimate embraces in the pits beyond the town. He feels the avid pacing of dogs like the pattering of his own heart. He sees soil in half open eyes and hears the small liquid clicking of the onset of decay, the movement of a blind beetle across the gape of a blackened wound. He lies like a mirror, reflecting the void. The window is still black. He closes his eyes and thinks of Pasiphae's reflection in a polished copper mirror. In some other room in the brain which is the palace, she stares unblinking into her own eyes. The round pupils gaze, begin to undulate as if the mirror were black water. His eyes flick open. The room is moving, rising and shuddering, like a ship climbing the long swell of the sea. A wine glass slides off the table by the bed and smashes, and then the bottle tilts and falls. The spilt wine trembles redly on the tiles of the floor. Somewhere, a child screams. The bottle rolls backwards and forwards across the floor.

The world is a heeling ship. He lies, his hands gripping the edge of the bed frame, his heart gripping his throat, waiting for it to end: and it does, as if it had never happened. The room sighs back into stillness, achieves its necessary and utter motionlessness once more, rests. Is my eye open or shut, am I waking or in dream? The spilt wine is still. In the window the first thought of dawn pales the black.

As he crosses the courtyard in the leaden light of daybreak he catches sight of her standing in the shadows, wrapped in heavy furs, the cowled figures of her women just visible behind, black on black. He speaks.

"There is something I have to say, even though I know how you will reply. There was a tremor in the earth an hour ago. There may be more. The bull dancers say that the white bull grows violent and unpredictable at these times. Don't go to the bull now, not today."

She smiles at him, a small tight lipped smile which has something in it of domesticity, uxoriousness even.

"Since you know what my reply is going to be, perhaps we should get on."

He leads the way through darkened passageways and down the long ramp to the underground chamber. Her women follow like dead souls. The subterranean darkness is rank with the smell of the bull. She stands watching the darkness ebb as Daedalus lights the new lamps in their brackets one after another so that the light grows steadily and stealthy shadows retreat. The sound of the restless movement of the unseen bull echoes around the place. Pasiphae walks over to the wicker cow where it stands. A block of masonry has fallen from the roof vault in the night and lies on the newly sanded floor casting a dozen shadows. There is a faint haze of dust in the air.

He beckons to the queen's women and leads them into one of the side vaults. "Take this," he says, handing over a bundle of canvas, "it can be opened up into a kind of litter, in case the queen cannot walk... and here, take these pine torches. Light them if you need to fend off the bull as you leave. I shall not be able to pen it up again, once it is released," he says with oracular precision. Their apprehension is a palpable thing, like a taste in the mouth.

He walks back to Pasiphae and unfastens the back of the wicker cow, lifting it away to reveal the upholstered complexity within. It is cushioned and padded as if it were meant to keep her safe from the weight of the world itself and bespeaks his aching desire to save her. He turns to her and the furs drop from her shoulders. She is naked and wears no jewellery. Her hair is tied up as if she were a servant girl. I shall have to lift you, he says, stooping and clasping her around the thighs, his forearms beneath her buttocks, and lifts her from the ground. There is a brief struggle as she finds her position within the cow, knees apart, crouched. Her body is impassive in his grasp. There is nothing of desire or fear under his hands, just a rounded and familiar warmth. Is this her ecstasy of passivity? In giving herself over to the possible has she passed through the mirror and become some other self which yet remains unchanged? Is she now indistinguishable from the world, not to be divided from it, gone out into all of its possibilities? Have the lineaments of her body gone out into the world and become one with it? What might such thoughts mean? He does not know, cannot think, will never follow.

He picks up the curved section of basket work from the ground and places it over her, refastening the straps. He does not catch her eye. They do not speak.

He walks away to where the cow is penned. The straw of her stall is a mess of liquid shit. Her eyes roll and her hooves tread the mire in agitation as he smears away the mucus from her vent with his hand. He lifts his hand and sniffs at it.

It is eighteen paces from the door of the cow's stall to the wicker cow. As his foot falls forward into the eleventh pace the sand beneath its falling moves sideways and he stumbles. There is a noise such as you might hear in the hold of a ship as it grinds against the harbour wall. He kneels, waiting, but time begins again and he gets up.

He wipes away the mucus on the leather folds of the simulacrum and walks away again. He is a planet, an asteroid on the long elliptical orbit of desire, arrowing out into darkness.

The bronze bolts of the bull pen are newly forged. He puts down the heavy wineskin which is filled with oil. Next to it he places an unlit pine torch and a lighted lamp. He kneels to roll up the wick of the lamp so that the flame rises a little, going forward in his mind along the forking paths of possibility. He has not seen the bull, knows nothing. He draws the bolts and pulls the door away, standing behind it, out of the bull's line of sight, aware of the smell of new wood.

The bull passes out like a wall, a monstrous engine of fate, its pizzle already distending. There is no doubt, no slack. Its passing is a furrow turning under the plough, an advancing wave of the possible folding over into actuality.

It stops, splay footed like a fighting bull, head up, horns upswept in the sign of the double axe, the red sword unsheathing beneath its belly to the pulse of its blood.

With all the certainty, all the disclosed truth of a story told from its end to its beginning, the bull moves toward the queen's ark. Daedalus sees it mount his creature as if through heavy rain, watches the hooves tread and settle to thrust. Vision slows and thickens as the swagged abdomen clenches and drives the future forward through the fragile fence of the present. The floor of the bull court begins to move, as if the waves of the sea were passing beneath it. The world slews, foundering. Unmaking oceans boom and roar. The bull is plucked away from the cow, a toy thrown from the crib, crashing sideways in an explosion of sand like the wreckage of a cart. Daedalus lies gasping in the lift of the swell. Through the oarhole of his eye he watches the bull rise again from the sea, staggering, its broken member a red stick hanging beneath it. Out of his prescient dreams the magician foresees the lowering of the horns, the driving hook upward and to the left. The lower horn splinters through the cow's flank with a tearing motion and the whole frail wickerwork structure jolts violently to one side. Daedalus knows two things: he knows that the horn has missed Pasiphae's body and he knows that the bull is just beginning its work. He discovers himself running across the sand in a rain of falling stone, whirling the flaming torch to incandescence. The horns are going down again. Daedalus bursts the wineskin of oil open against the wall of its flank in a great shower as the white bull piles forward in that same iterated and dreamed of upsweep. The cow goes over, skids as the horns drive it. The bull shakes itself free of the splintered mess and backs away, hooves pawing. The horns go down again. Daedalus steps in and sets fire to the bull, holding the torch against its panting bulk. The oil soaked hide shrivels and catches. Flames and black smoke erupt.

The world slows again as the burning bull spins, a wheel of fire turning on the axis of the man. The golden horns pass before his face like stately ships. He marks every scratch and chip and gilded glint with the clarity of a dreamer. Arabesques of flame roil redly in the slow thunderheads of black smoke that billow from the burning flesh.

Pain brings him to. His scorched tunic smoulders against his skin and he tears it from his body in sudden panic, stands naked in the smoke. Somewhere the wreckage of the flaming bull crashes and bellows. Women pass close by him in the fog and he finds his frenzied fingers unfastening the straps of the ruined cow. Pasiphae falls limply away like a stillborn infant. There is blood. They bundle her into the canvas shroud and stagger, stooping under its weight, across the convulsing rubble, weaving and stumbling under their burden. A block of masonry falls from the ceiling in a shower of dust, soundless in the roaring dark, felling the leading figure with no slowing of its descent, so that the whole group go down in confusion and hysteria. The ship of the world is foundering in smoke and noise and darkness.

18

"I knew the girl was dead and I knew that Pasiphae was alive in the same instant. You could hardly see for the smoke. My eyes were streaming and I was groping about among the fallen bodies of the women. I felt the slab of stone that had fallen from the roof. She was still beneath it. It lay across her shoulders and the back of her head. I could just make out her face. Her eyes were open. I thought she was looking at me but her head was crushed. And at the same time underneath me Pasiphae moved. I'd been kneeling on her. And then the bull passed over us up the ramp. You know I don't think we would have got out of that place if the bull hadn't gone up that ramp like a torch as if it was lighting the way..."

Daedalus winces as the fisherman's wife smears his reddened and blistered skin with the strong smelling stuff she has brought.

"Go on."

"I don't know what happened. We were outside somehow. One of the women had had the back of her clothing ripped away when the bull went over us. I think some of her ribs were broken. There was a hoofprint in the middle of her back, like some mark of evil. Outside, it was chaos. The ground was still shaking. Fires were burning. There were people everywhere, shouting and screaming and running about......"

He winces again.

"Sorry. What about the queen?"

"They pulled back the canvas from her face. She wasn't conscious but she was breathing. There was nothing to be done. We just sat there in a huddle until the ground stopped moving and then they got up and took her away, the women."

"You didn't go with them?"

"I'd started to cry by then. They just got up and left."

Daedalus begins to weep again.

19

Dog days of aftermath. The earthquake passes like the passing of a fever. Tremors ripple for weeks, growing less and less. Days of fearful anticipation wane into days of apathy. The thunder of the distant volcano grows less as the days unfold and the infernal sound passes out of consciousness. Only in the silence of the night, when the sleeper awakes from some formless nightmare, can it be heard echoing out of Tartarus.

The damage to the palace and to the town of Cnossus is extensive. Much that survived the earthquake has been destroyed by the fires which broke out in the ruins. Much survives. A stork's nest sits serene on a crumbling pinnacle of the only remaining wall of the temple. The bird lofts away and back unperturbed.

Death has come strangely. A collapsing stairwell has carried away a clutch of the king's courtiers. One of the queen's women died under a falling stone. Many have died in their beds under falling walls. Those who rose early on that day were able to run out into the buckling streets and survived. Many who slept, died.

There is a half-formed feeling among the survivors that retribution has somehow been exacted, that they have somehow been let off lightly in the matter of the refugees, and few are tempted to rail against fate. It is a place in the collective consciousness of the town which is marked by pauses in speech, by moments of vacancy. The work of repair begins in a spirit of hesitant contrition. There is speech now where there was evasion and the averting of eyes. The people of Cnossus have forgiven themselves because they believe the blood price has been paid. The embroidered tale of the burning bull in the palace becomes bound up with stories of the divine origin of the earthquake itself. The leaning façade of the temple below the stork's nest is piled with flowers. There is talk of building a new temple.

The charred wreckage of the bull was found in the bull leapers practise court, they say, with its horns buried in the magician's wooden bull. When Daedalus hears this gossip he knows that his life is no more than a blown feather. His shadow goes before him down the street like bad luck. A woman comes down to his workshop in the port. He recognises her as one of Pasiphae's women, one of those who were with her in the underground hall.

"The queen wishes you to know that she is making a recovery. She will send for you when she is well."

The woman pulls her cowl around her face and hurries away.

The port has suffered strangely. A tidal wave as high as a house came out of the horizon in the mid-morning of that day, drowning fifty souls. The town square, two hundred yards from the sea is deep in wrack and splintered boats. On the edge of town a rowing boat sits in the top of a tree. Daedalus has hurried out along the beach as fast as his burned skin will allow to find news of his son. The boy is well and beams up from his work mending the nets when his father says his name. "We were at sea," Sinon tells Daedalus, "which was a fortunate thing. The wave passed beneath us before it broke. It was as if the ship were climbing a mountain. We were lucky. Boats and lives have been lost. It is heavy work," he says wryly, "living through the end of the world."

20

Naucrate sits up holding the king's wax seal on its ribbon between her naked breasts.
"Why now? What does he want?"
"Who knows what Minos wants?"
"Why does he want to see you? And why now?"
"I cannot penetrate the mind of a madman. My stomach aches, which is not a good sign."
"Is he really mad? I am afraid for you."
"So am I."
"When must you go?"
"Tonight. I shall walk up to the palace. I should leave soon."
She looks into his face and his grey eyes meet hers. He says,
"You know that they found the burned bull dead with its horns buried in the wooden bull I made for the bull court. That fact is on his mind. He is in trouble. If these earthquakes begin again then the people will be looking for a sacrifice, some way of propitiating the Mother. In the old days, long ago, the king was king only for a season and at the end of his season of kingship he was sacrificed to the Mother for the good of all. It is not a custom he would like to see revived, I think. He is afraid of Pasiphae. In her person she is Io the moon cow as he is the bull, but she is also the snake mother and in these days of fear people are turning again to the Mother. Her altar in the grove has been piled with flowers for weeks. Minos knows that Pasiphae has come here, to the workshop. He knows at least that much. Perhaps he knows more."
He gets up and pulls her to her feet but he does not let go of her hands. He looks at the backs of her hands as they rest in his own, the tapering fingers, the nails pale against the sunburned skin. He looks at her body.
"I am glad you come here, Naucrate. I am grateful for what has passed between us. I shall be sorry when it ends."

They begin collecting their clothes together from the floor. He stands on one leg fastening his sandal by the opening that looks out over the sea. Two slave ships move out toward the horizon under sail. He says,

"You know, there is a thing I have wondered about..."

She looks at him as she brushes her hair.

"Your husband. Does your husband know you come here?"

"Yes. I tell him. And I tell him what we do together. I like to tell him and he likes to listen. Sometimes I make things up."

Daedalus' face is a picture.

"There, Daedalus the Athenian, that will give you something else to think about as you walk to the palace, apart from whether the king will cut off your head. You are not the only person in the world."

She crosses toward the ladder and is about to descend.

"There is something else you might like to think about. I know that before she coupled with the bull, the queen sent you her ring and that you returned it to her in person. She sent her ring to me too, on a different night, and I also returned it to her, in person."

He listens as she passes down the long ladders and out of earshot.

21

The year has turned. Purple Summer has passed into grey Autumn. In the port, stinging slingshots of cold rain drive across the market place. The stallholders are chilled, wet and bad tempered. Business is slow and they pass the time grumbling, their hands wafered under their armpits, stamping their feet. There remains a feeling of dereliction, as at the end of a war. Debris from the great wave still lies in drifts of wrack against the walls of the houses around. Some wag is selling vegetables out of the wreckage of a boat. The place is half empty, the produce poor and expensive. Many stalls are untenanted. There are gaunt strangers among the familiar faces, beggars, foreigners. Women buy what they need and hurry home to their warm hearths, out of the rain. The beadseller is hawking his fish among the stallholders. He has become a familiar face and the traders respond despite themselves to his amiable good manners and his curiously formal accent. Already he has exchanged a squid for a piece of goats' cheese so that his professional honour is satisfied, sufficiently anyway for such a cold wet day. Mostly it is barter: fish in exchange for bread or eggs or whatever is to be had, sometimes a little money. He pulls his shawl about his head against a sudden gust of rain and it occurs to him that he will walk back now to the shipyard, picturing the bright fire twinkling in the inventor's workshop.

As he is leaving the market square he passes a boy who is squatting on the wet kerbside with a piece of cloth laid out in front of him on the ground. On the cloth glass beads are set out in rows. The beadseller squats on his hams to examine the paltry merchandise. He picks up a bead. It is large, lozenge shaped, pierced through its shorter axis, pale green, opalescent. He places it in his palm and holds it very close to his face because his eyes are still bad, a little worse maybe.

"Egyptian, as I am sure you know. I once travelled to the village where they make these particular beads. A place of little huts. An ancient craft in that place. Very distinctive, don't you think? I am a beadseller myself. It is good to meet another who is engaged in the trade."

He holds out his hand and the boy takes it. The hand is thin and chill, the boy famished, far gone in privation, but unbowed. He meets the beadseller's eye candidly.

"How much would you take for this piece?

The boy is agog, his stare blank.

"I have here a small parcel of goat's cheese, a little overripe perhaps but good, good. Ripeness is a virtue in cheese. When I was a boy my father refused to drink milk until it was sour, claiming that it was unripe. What do you think?"

He offers the boy a small piece to try and it is gone in a moment. The boy's face wears a look of avid, doglike expectancy.

"A third, say. What would you say to a third part of this cheese in exchange for the Egyptian bead? Does that seem fair? What do you think?"

The boy nods, speechless, as the beadseller breaks off the cheese and hands it over. It disappears into the boy's mouth in the time it takes for the beadseller to wrap up the remainder. The old man stands, a little stiffly. Rain rakes the pavement.

"A pleasure to do business with you. Perhaps, if you are here tomorrow... there are some blue pieces, these ones, that I may be interested in. Do you like bread? Tomorrow I may have bread. Good afternoon."

He takes the boy's hand again with formal courtesy, pockets his bead and leaves the rainy market square.

22

The king's torturers sit gravely watching as Daedalus enters the royal chamber. They are pilgrims who have wandered long in the forests of the blood, who have entered the souls of men through bleeding rags of flesh, through the crushed conduit of the bone. They have stood the watch impassively through blood boltered nights, have steered their vessels home to the harbour of the dying heart. They sit like mariners who have returned from unknown continents, in the silence of what they have seen and done.

Daedalus stands before Minos. Behind the throne, Talos the king's giant stands, his brass limbs unmoving. He is twice the size of a man. He might be mistaken for a colossal statue, save that his eyelids blink from time to time. Minos lowers the bull mask from his face, letting the moment distend, full of menace.

"I have been thinking for a long time of having you killed. But then you will know that already. It is well known that you traffic with the dead. I had thought to load you and all of the devices and engines and mannikins which you have made, with chains and to burn everything in that ruin where you work. But I held back. I was afraid that I might miss something and that one of your creatures would survive to avenge you. These gentlemen here have agreed to put you to the question. They tell me that when they have finished their work there will remain no sinew or secret space in your body wherein the smallest evasion could hide. They tell me that you will plead, beg, to reveal all of your works, and at the end, that you will weep like an infant for the release of death."

The king pauses in his speech. Daedalus is trying not to let his legs tremble. His bladder threatens to betray him. That part of him which perches in the rafters of the royal chamber can see the forking path, can smell the indecision which Minos gives off like the smell of sweat. That part of him which stands on the marble floor beneath, clenching his fluttering bowels, is intent only upon holding himself together. There are two birds in the cosmic tree. Minos begins again. The pitch of his voice has risen, grown sharp.

"You will also know that in the recent visitation the white bull was consumed by a thunderbolt while attempting to destroy the wooden engine built in its likeness by you. I summoned the priests of the palace to see this portent, and of course they could not agree if it was a warning. Some thought it a warning, some a favourable omen. They argued about what it meant, bickering like schoolboys. I am surrounded by babbling idiots. I am practised upon by rogues and charlatans!'

Minos is shouting now, his self possession leaking away, on the edge of tears.

"There is no one to help me. Who is helping you, Athenian? Which God guards you and your works? Why are you my enemy? Are they right? Are you my enemy? I believe you are. There are only enemies."

There are tears running down his cheeks. He continues to speak, his voice breaking into a parody of amiable intimacy.

"They tell me you can fly. Is that true?"

Daedalus opens his mouth as if he would reply but the king's voice rises to a sudden girlish shriek.

"Silence! Silence! Do not speak! The sound of your voice could be fatal to me!"

Minos hobbles down, trailing his gilded bull mask, to where the magician stands. His tear streaked face comes close. His voice shudders with sobbing.

"I shall have you watched. I shall find your secret. I shall intercede with your god. I shall find a way to be rid of you."

The magician's body grows calm. He finds that he has passed through the dark place and stands in the sunlit afternoon of what he knows and does not know, listening to the close, sobbing breathing. He turns and walks out of the chamber. The broken voice echoes after him.

"I shall find a way. I shall find a way."

23

It is a better day in the town square, though still cold. Racing patches of sunlight and cloudshadow follow one another over the flapping awnings of the market stalls and the piled vegetables. The old man is aware of the boy over in the far corner of the square but he takes his time trading the red mullet they caught yesterday, fishing from the beach with the long weighted lines. The inventor's gift to them of hooks and lines has given the little group a new life. Where once they were merchants or retired vintners or tyrannical matriarchs they are now fisherfolk, able to eke a living of sorts. The beadseller takes his time, loitering here and there to gossip. He exchanges the catch for flour, olives, bread, a little money, and finally he passes the boy again sitting in the same spot, his cloth and his beads before him.

"And how is business today, my friend?"

In spite of his distressed condition there is something about the boy, some hint of satisfaction in the contours of his face. The old man guesses that he is twelve, maybe thirteen years old.

"I sold some beads. I made a sale."

He holds out a palm full of small change.

"It is a fine thing, to make a sale. There is a satisfaction in a bargain well struck. For the buyer and the seller."

"An old woman who spoke strangely. She had a face like an eagle and white hair like a cloud."

The boy gestures the volume of her hair with his hands and grimaces her expression.

"She said I should use some of this money to buy strips of leather so that I could make up bracelets and necklaces. She said it would be good for business. But I am very hungry and I think I shall have to spend the money on food."

"She was a wise woman. And I have been thinking about those blue beads, you know. Indeed I could hardly sleep for thinking about them. I have here some fine olives and some loaves of bread. Bread and olives. What more can a man ask from life? Maybe we too could strike a bargain."

The old man and the boy discuss the relative merits of the beads and the bread at length as they squat across from one another on the pavement. The beadseller imparts the courtesies and the ploys of the merchant's craft by example in his conversation and the boy is quick to understand, to imitate. There is an ease in the boy's nature, undimmed by privation.

The boy chews on a piece of the bread which the beadseller has given him so that he can assess its quality, and a handful of olives purely for the purpose of testing their flavour. The boy tries to eat slowly, the very soul of judicious consideration. The old man examines the rows of beads as he eats.

"This is a fine collection, one might almost say, a regal collection. These are not beads you would find around the neck of a farmer's wife. Where does a man come by such a collection as this?"

The boy stops chewing and his face grows clouded but he meets the old man's gaze frankly.

"I didn't steal them but I am not sure if they are really mine."

The old man inclines his head sympathetically, inviting him to continue. The boy thinks for a minute.

"It will be best if I start at the beginning. My father makes pots. It is our family business. We live in Gournia. Do you know Gournia? They say the town fell down in the earthquakes. I don't know. It's a long time since I was there. You see, I am the youngest. I am one of seven brothers and there wasn't going to be a place in our business for me, not with six older brothers in the same business and so, about a year ago my father sent me to work on the farm of his uncle, but I didn't like it. My father's uncle was a hard master. His wife had died and he lived alone. He never laughed or told a joke, and so I left and walked to Cnossus. It was a long walk and I don't know why I thought of going there. I had heard the name. I knew that the Minos lived there. I found work in the palace, in the stables cleaning harnesses and polishing chariots and litters and the other fine things that belonged to the king and queen. Beautiful things they were, all shiny wood and polished copper and glass beads.

The queen had a parasol which was kept there, a great big umbrella with long fringes made from beads. And heavy. Someone used to carry it for her when she went out walking. One day I was given the job of carrying it. Someone had fallen sick and they said I had to do it. I had to wear different clothes that went with the parasol on the days when I had to carry it and they were heavy as well. Too big for me and they had a funny smell. The queen is a very fine lady but she frightened me and it was so hard to keep her in the shade of the parasol when she went out walking in the sun. I was afraid I would bump into her. It was like carrying a tree about. You couldn't stop straight away. This chamberlain, he said, "do it like this, stand like this, hold it like this," but I don't think he'd ever had a go at it himself. It was easier if it was a special occasion, even though lots of people were watching, because then she would walk slowly but at other times she would stop suddenly, just when you weren't expecting it, or go sideways even. Sometimes she ran. It was a very hard job keeping her in the shade. I sometimes used to wonder if she cared whether she was in the shade or not. I used to wish she would help me a bit, you know, go slowly and not do anything sudden but I don't think she even noticed if I was there at all.

I used to have this dream where I would say to the queen, I would say, "Excuse me, your majesty, but would you mind walking more slowly and in straight lines and if you're going to turn will you give me a signal to let me know which way you're going to go. It's important for your skin, to keep it out of the sun. I'm only doing it for your own good." And she would say, "What a sensible boy," and after that she would put out her hand if she was going to turn, her left hand if she was going left and her other hand if she was going the other way. She had a signal for stop too, and another one for when she was going to go again. It was just a dream.

On the day of the earthquake I was lucky. I was already up and about. I was in one of the palace kitchens. There was an old woman who used to make really good barley cakes but you had to be up early. So when the earthquake started I was in this kitchen, and me and the old woman ran outside and we were all right, and, you know, when it was over she opened her apron and it was full of warm barley cakes. A lot of the palace had fallen down and fires were burning and people were crying and screaming, and we sat there eating barley cakes.

I hung around for a day or two but it seemed like a bad luck place after the earthquake. Some of the people I knew had been killed. The chamberlain who had showed me about the parasol, he'd been killed. I wasn't sorry, not really. A lot of people left. They just went away. I went back to the part of the palace where I worked and it was just rubble. I thought I'd made a mistake at first and come to the wrong place. There was hardly anybody about. Someone said the queen was sick and I thought, well, she won't be going out and about if she's sick. There wasn't much of anything left in that part of the palace. There'd been this fire, but in the ash and the rubbish I spotted a bead, and I recognised it. Sounds silly, doesn't it, but I did. It was a big blue one that hung at the very end of one of the tassels on the queen's parasol, sort of curled, like a shell, but not quite the same as all the others. I raked about a bit and I found hundreds, thousands of them. All the cloth and everything had burnt away but the beads were still there. At first I just collected them, like you do. It reminded me of when I was little, when I used to collect ladybirds. I used to collect smooth stones too, white ones, when I was about six. Anyway, I didn't stop until it got dark, I just went on for hours raking through the ashes with a stick and picking up the beads. In the end I had this big pile. I spent ages looking for something to put them in, and then I found this old bucket and I put the beads in the bucket and I left. I just carried the beads for company. It was dark you see, on the road out of town. You could see the moon shining on the sea far away. And then I had this thought as I was walking in the dark. Do you know what I thought? I thought I'd come here to the market. I've been here before, carrying these beads when they were still in the parasol. The queen used to go down to the shipyards to see her magician. Anyway I had this sort of dream as I was walking down the road from the palace. I dreamt that I would come here to the market and sell the beads and use the money to sail away in a ship. I've never been on a ship. They're not all here you know, the beads. I hid a lot of them. I thought I might get robbed."

A silence falls between them. The boy's gaze moves absently across the square. The beadseller wonders how to proceed. At last he asks,

"Where do you sleep?"

"In a boat on the beach. Under the nets. It's cold at night."

"In the place where I stay, in the shipyard, there are some people who used to live in Gournia. They may have news of your family. There is a fire there."

"A fire?"

24

"I am quick with life," Pasiphae smiles up at him from her bed, wan, ironic, "though I am not certain yet where the responsibility lies, with the bull, or with you."

Daedalus is shocked by her sunken appearance. Her eyes are dark. The contours of her body as she lies beneath the sumptuous stuffs of the bed, are the contours of pain.

"But it has been a hard beginning."

Slowly and with care she pulls back the coverlet and lifts the dressing from her leg. The wound is an angry, weeping crater in the flesh of her thigh. The horn has pierced the tattooed snake below its head. Her thigh is hugely swollen and yellow around the livid hole. He senses the heat of infection and she catches his thought.

"I may yet die of this, but I think not. It is better than it was."

She covers herself again, wincing, and sinks back exhausted against the pillows. She looks up at him as he stands over the bed and their eyes lock.

"You have killed my passion, magician, you have sent him into the flames."

"It would have killed you."

"He may have killed me yet."

"What else could I do?"

"What else? You are as much the creature of your nature as I am. Burning the white bull has brought you close to the brink. Minos wants you dead. He has wanted you dead a long time, but he is afraid to have you killed now in case he too goes into the flames. He wishes he had done it sooner, before the times slipped out of joint. He thinks that the bull was killed by a bolt of lightning, and that is the reason you are alive. If he knew the truth you would not be here. He believes his fate is caught up in the fate of the bull. He believes its death has weakened him, that it was a warning from God. He fears he may die of it."

"How much does he know?"

"Everything and nothing. He hears voices, some real, some not. The clamour in his head is ceaseless and he does not know which voice to attend to or where the truth lies. You could rule him. He would listen to your voice. He is afraid of you."

"It is not what I want."

"If you do not choose to rule him he will find the courage to kill you in the end. He will not let you leave. I cannot save you. Perhaps I shall not be able to save myself. I have lost sight of who you are, magician, but I believe that Minos does well to be afraid of you."

He kneels on the floor by the bed and lays his head by her on the covers. She reaches out her hand, curls his hair absently around her fingers for loss and abandonment and the weariness that lies at the end of everything. The room grows dim, the crepuscular light thickens as the late afternoon drains toward evening. They sleep. Time passes. Outside, the wind of winter is rising. She wakes.

"You must go."

As he crosses the twilit courtyards the wind drives leaves in rattling vortices around his legs. Overhead, the indigo night is still streaked with livid daylight.

25

He has cleared a wide space in the workshop. Workbenches are stacked atop one another against the walls. Baskets and boxes and all the dusty paraphernalia of his calling are heaped carelessly in tottering piles out of the way. The big articulated puppets sprawl across this debris like corpses.

He has built a floor in this cleared space. A floor of smooth planks nailed to long wooden joists, chocked and supported over the worn, uneven flags of the stone floor beneath. It is like a dancefloor, planed, level, exact, and across its surface is painted a huge and complex diagram, a veined scimitar of black lines.

He is kneeling at the centre of this web, hammering nails into the wood at intervals along the painted lines, not driving the nails home but leaving them standing a finger's length proud of the surface. The bronze nails which lie about him dance with each hammerblow. Every little while he puts his eye to the floor to check his work and then taps the side of a nail to bring it to plumb vertical or drives one a little further home so that it lies level with its fellows.

Naucrate has come in, unseen, and stands to one side watching him work, her brow furrowed. She cannot make sense of the painted lines and even when she walks around the four sides of the raised wooden floor her view remains too oblique for her to fathom the intersecting curves of the drawing. He kneels with his hammer at the centre, unaware of her, absorbed in the job. She will not ask and it irritates her that she cannot make sense of what he is doing. Finally she goes over to the long ladder and ascends to a place which overlooks the workshop. She looks down to the floor, forty feet below. He is kneeling at the centre of a wing, the skeletal wing of a dragon or a huge bat. The great pinions curve outward, clawlike, and are connected, one to another, by an elaborate tracery of lesser lines. He is dwarfed by it. The fixity of his purpose seems inhuman to her. It is what she fears in him, and yet what draws her to him. There is something childlike, she thinks, in his blindness to the limits of the possible. He kneels like a spider at the centre of a web, working, working, immune to doubt it seems, in the candle flicker of his mortality, blind to the possibility of failure. She calls down, her voice belying her feelings, mocking him,

"You won't fly far with only one wing."

"Wing? It's a fly swatter. In case we have a plague of giant flies. I think one just flew in."

When she returns to the ground, he stands up, knees stiff.

"Why nails?"

"To bend the strips of wood around to make the shape of the wings. Come, I'll show you."

He walks before her, leading her through the jagged hole that will never be a door to the space where the wicker cow once stood, and there, hanging from a dozen threads in the small light of oil lamps, is the delicately boned skeleton of a small dragon. It is suspended in a reverie of flight, more like a dragonfly, perhaps, than a dragon, in its fragile lucent complexity. The fine silk which is stretched in a membrane and finely stitched over its spidery integuments, is almost transparent. The dark space is a temple to its frail, unbreathing beauty. Even in its stillness it exists in that space between what is made and what is born. Beneath the wings, close to the place where its heart might be, sits a small jointed figure of a man, in a cat's cradle of threads and pedals. She stands, rapt before its alien beauty.

He takes her over to where the threaded skeleton of a seabird tilts, a spectral bird planing down the locked wind.

"See the breastbone, how deep it is, like the keel of a ship. The muscles of the wings are anchored to that bone. It is the hardest thing to enter in to the forces that play along that bone, to be in the bird, to feel the hawser pull of the wind under the wings. Gliding is not so difficult to understand. I can make a thing to glide. I can trim it to turn, to catch the updraught, to go down the wind, but I do not know if it is possible to make a machine that rows the air like a bird. There is a world in the downstroke of a bird's wing. When I try to make a simulacrum of that wingbeat, materials fail, will not withstand the necessary forces and yet be light enough. Joints rend and will not hold together. And where is the strength in a man that will match those fearful muscles? Perhaps I can make a machine that will fly once, that will expend its nature in a single flight."

"You are a man, not a bird."

"I shall need to find a way to leave this island, to escape Minos."

"You could escape his anger by ship. You could disguise yourself as another. You could evade him. You are cunningly wrought Daedalus, you could slip through the world's net unseen."

She walks to the jagged doorway. He says,

"I am watched. You know that."

"Is this private? Do Minos' spies not see this?"

She waves her arm angrily out toward the huge drawing on the wooden platform.

"It is your folly, Daedalus, to believe yourself greater, cleverer than you are. Minos fears you are a god in disguise and deep down you believe his madness. It is your vanity. There is no time for all this. You must go now. Minos will come for you. He will come soon."

She is crying now, crying out of the knowledge that he cannot be saved, that he is the unseeing slave of his condition, his sex. She runs out of the place, past the firelit shapes of the refugees. He stands immobile, watching her disappear into the gloom, the hammer hanging in his hand, in the dark emptiness of his workshop. He knows that he will never know, that he only understands from the inside, like a prisoner fingering the walls of his cell as he dreams of a world beyond. He returns to his work.

26

"Thrace is wild and bare. The winters are bad. I remember snow in the wind, icicles hanging from the eaves. On cold mornings your breath hung like a cloud in the air. Here you only see snow on distant mountaintops. Here winters are poor affairs, a few weeks of wind and rain. Cretans get so bad tempered in the winter, but it is hardly a winter at all. They shouldn't complain. The warmth here is good. When you are growing old it is better than snow, better than watching your breath freeze on your collar."

Oenone's mane of white hair is haloed red as she stoops over the fire to pour the soup and her features are silhouetted against the flames. Outside, the night wind is blowing. She passes a steaming bowl to the beadseller and bread to go with it. He sits before the fire with the bowl in his cupped hands.

"It is good to sit in a house when it grows dark and the wind is blowing."

He eats what she has given him and she watches him eat.

"I think about Thrace more and more as I grow older. Little things come back to me. Things from childhood I thought I had forgotten. A wooden doll that used to be my mother's when she was a girl, and her mother's before that. It's limbs had joints that were fastened together with string. I remember watching my mother mend it when one of the arms came off. I can remember my grandmother, though she died when I was still a tiny girl, tall and bony she was, like a carving, hands like mine are now."

Oenone turns her strong, old woman's hands in the firelight.

"But it is all memory now. Our village was burned, the people carried off into slavery. Nothing remains, except memory. It is as if I have lived two lives. There was life before the slave ships came and there was life after. Before they came I had a husband, grown sons, a house, neighbours, fields to till. It was a life, complete, and now I have another. Crete was strange to me when I came here, a name on the lips of a sailor, a land where a brass giant lived and a bull ruled as king, and now it is home. It is where I live. I have a house, neighbours, a bar on the waterfront to run.

Sometimes I walk past the warehouse where we were kept. It is still the same. I know the cages inside are still used. The trade still goes on. Once I saw a line of captives, chained together, being herded through the door. They did not chain us when they first brought us here. We were all too weak to make trouble. The voyage had been bad. It is a long voyage from the north. The ship with my husband and sons on it sank in a storm. I found out later. People died in those cages too, in that warehouse. I did not care whether I lived or died so it was easy for me. I pitied those with children. Many of the children died.

A man came one day and bought a child. It was the day before I was set free. I think maybe it was him who paid my price. Later, months, maybe a year later, he came into a bar where I was working, that man. I said to him, "You bought a child from the slave traders. Did you buy me too?" It was as if I were an orphan child seeking a parent, a name. He said to me, "You are mistaken, it must have been another." But I was not mistaken. I see him once in a while. He drinks in the bars along the harbourside.

It was a strange thing when they set me free, like a dream. They came to the cage where I was. "Which is Oenone?" they said. I was afraid and I didn't answer at first. They took me out and led me to the door of that place. "Go', they said, "Someone has paid your price. You are free." I stood outside in the sunshine. I remember it, everything. It was like being born. I sat against the wall outside that warehouse, in the warm sunshine. I had been given back to myself. It was a mystery. I did not think about those who were still inside. I still do not know what became of them, and yet they were my life, the people in those cages, all that I had known, and I walked away from that place as if they had never existed. I think about that man who came to buy the child. Why did he want a child? He said it was for a rich family who had lost their baby. Which family? Why did he pay my price? I used to think about following him one night, finding out who he is. But then, even if I knew, what would I know? The mystery of the human heart would still be a mystery. It is all a long time ago now."

They sit, staring into the fire. At last he says,

"The boy is better here with you. It is better to live in a house."

"He is a good boy, an honest nature. I feed him, help him with his bracelets, not much. Do you mind?"

"He is better here. It is better for him here than camping like a gypsy in the shipyards. The winter is coming on. Though it is true, I enjoyed his company. As you say, he will become an honest man, and he has a merchant's gifts. He will do well, I think, though he will need to replenish his little stock of beads soon. He is saving his money."

The embers of the fire collapse and the room brightens for a moment. They sit at either side of the hearth, listening to the wind in the chimney. Beyond the harbour lights the sea stretches to black infinity. Out on the dark sea there is no ship, no light. She looks up into his face and he returns her gaze myopically. Somewhere outside in the darkness a shutter is banging in the wind. The old woman says,

"You are right, the winter is coming on."

The beadseller sits for a long time in silence, turning the empty soupbowl in his hands.

27

He is coming in to land and he knows he is going too fast. The shadow of the great sailwing grows ever larger as it sweeps across the hillside below him. He hauls on the handlines but he has not the strength left in his arms to bring it up into a stall and the whole spidery apparatus piles into the ground in a grinding confusion of splintering wood and tearing fabric.

He sits nursing the agony in his ankle and contemplates the smoke-dust which rises from the wreckage like a cloud.

"Shit, shit, shit, shit."

Twenty yards away a goat watches out of its slit eyes in blank astonishment. Grass hangs out at either side of its mouth. It dodges away, panic-stricken as Icarus appears over the hillside, carrying his wings on his head like a porter, having made the long glide from the summit without mishap. Delight is written on his face. When he approaches the ruins of his father's wings his brow furrows. Daedalus says,

"Here, give me a hand."

He winces as the boy pulls him to his feet.

"And this is just gliding. We've got to make something that flies."

28

Daedalus limps up the beach. He can barely see his feet for the swirling sand which drives in the wind along the shore to the height of his knees. He passes a fox running in blind circles in the sandstorm. The running of the fox is urgent though its open eyes are caked with sand and it runs without sight.

The crew of the fishing boat are sitting around a driftwood fire under the drumming awning of an old sail. The red ochre cloth cracks in the wind and the smoke of the fire flies down the beach faster than you could run. Icarus smiles broadly at his father from where he sits on a lobster pot. His teeth are white enough and even enough to break your heart. Sinon eyes Daedalus' gimping approach without comment. He gestures him to a place by the fire.

"Poor weather for fishing."

Sinon lets the inanity pass.

"I need your help... when the wind drops. Do you know the Lasithi cliffs, the big white cliffs west from here?"

Sinon raises an eyebrow at the obvious question.

"How long does it take to sail there?"

"It depends. It depends on the wind."

It is Daedalus' turn to raise an eyebrow.

"Half a day."

"If I come to you on a day of my choosing at dawn, can you be at those cliffs by noon?"

Sinon nods, his brow heavy with unasked questions.

"I'll light a fire so that you will know where to anchor."

"I cannot anchor below those cliffs. The water is too deep."

"But you can stop?"

"I have a sea anchor."

"You will see me fly off the cliff. Some time after that I will land in the sea. I'll try to come down somewhere near the boat. I want you to be ready to fish me out, me and the wings. It is important that the wings are retrieved intact. Bring Icarus with you."

Sinon's face is a study in incomprehension.

"I'll pay you now."

Daedalus rummages under his cloak but the fisherman waves him away.

"Pay me later."

"I need a light wind from the north West."

"You would get such a wind on any Summer's day."

"I cannot wait for the Summer."

"The sea will be cold."

"There are worse things."

Sinon looks at him and shakes his head.

29

He lies on his stomach at the cliff edge looking down at the distant seethe of water among the shadowed rocks. In the middle airs, gulls circle and veer, crying mournfully. Panic flutters in his loins, but he indulges his fear, letting his eyes fall from the waving fronds of grass near his face, down the vertiginous white walls of the cliff, down to the remote, blue shadowed water. He squirms backward on his belly away from the cliff edge, and sits up. The horizon is empty. The wings lie a few yards away in the grass and he resists the impulse to check them over once again. Further off, rotten branches are piled up, with dry grass stuffed between, ready to be lighted when the boat appears. He has sent the cart back to the port, and he can see it now, breasting a distant rise of the grassy clifftop on its way back to the town. It is cold in the thin breeze and he stamps about, flapping his arms. He rummages in his bag and fishes out the bread he has brought. It is her bread, bread Naucrate has made, stale now. He holds it against his nose and his eyes fill with tears. Loss breaks over him like a wave. He knows that he is driving events to a conclusion that he does not want, that he does not even understand. It is all he knows how to do, to bring things to an end. It has always been the same. He makes things and steps over them, drawn to whatever comes next. He does not know how to change it. In the uncertain half light of his thought he sees the fisherman's wife. She is a glimmer of flesh, standing at the dark altar. He is afraid for her, for her and for Pasiphae, and there is need in him too, for comfort, rest. Yet he cannot find the means to turn aside from the path that will take him away from them, does not know how to form the thoughts that will break the pattern.

Yesterday, when Naucrate came to the workshop, he was ferreting in the piled debris of his trade. She cannot see him at first among the dusty mounds of boxes and crates. He calls out to her.

"I won't be a minute. There's something I want to show you,

something I've been working on for a long time."

He emerges with a box. He carries it across to where she is standing by the warmth of the brazier and sets it down. It is a deep box with handles, its bound corners fogged with rust. He blows the dust off the top and she watches as he fiddles with the catches. He lifts the lid clear and she crouches to look inside.

It is a sort of maze or ants' nest, a model with rooms and corridors, but tiny, an ant city.

"This is a model of Cnossus palace. There is Pasiphae's apartment, and look, that's the colonnade that runs past it, and that's the bull court, and the practice hall. Do you see those little spots of coloured paint? They mark the entrances to the lower levels. Watch."

He lifts away the palace, the top layer, to reveal another floor below, another maze.

"This is beneath the palace. Some of it is cellars, storerooms, and some of it is the remains of palaces built years ago. But look, there and there, those coloured spots mark the entrances to the level below."

He lifts away another tier and there beneath it is another warren of rooms and tunnels and stairs. He lifts away a third layer to reveal more of the labyrinth beneath.

"Is it real? Does all of this really lie beneath the palace?"

"Yes. Mostly it's what's left of ancient palaces, forgotten long ago, built over. I have changed some things. I still do it. Dassis, the chamberlain lets me use his masons when work is slack. I alter this model when we make changes to the labyrinth."

"How long? How long have you been doing this?"

"I don't know. Years. Since I arrived almost."

"Why?"

"What is there to say? It's a labyrinth, an image of the limits of thought. It stands for what comes after thinking."

"Why are you showing it to me?"

"You might need it. It's hard to know, hard to foresee all of the possibilities."

Daedalus is still standing with the bread pressed to his nose. Sinon's boat bobs in the shadow of the cliff.

30

Naucrate holds the tall stepladder steady as he installs himself in the web of ropes and straps and pulley wheels which hang beneath the dragon. The great outstretched wings are suspended in the void of the workshop, the skeletal pinions half lost in the gloom. She pulls the ladder away and returns to stand beneath him, craning up to where he hangs in his cat's cradle.

"This is how it will glide, like this, wings spread, locked off. This is what I already know. I can trim the glide, turn, stall. See. Icarus does it well."

She watches the broad profile of the wings evolve, moment to moment, as his hands move and she glimpses the ghost of the soaring gull in its subtle mechanical evolutions.

"But this, this, is different. I've tested it. It works."

"You've tested it?"

"Off the cliff at Lasithi."

"Off the cliff?"

He is oblivious to her incredulity.

"That's right. At Lasithi. Sinon fished me out of the water with his boat."

Her consternation takes another turn as the outstretched wings begin to fold without warning, as if they had broken at the centre. The wingtips rise majestically and Daedalus descends in a singing of pulley wheels until he sits a few feet above her, suspended at the lowest point of the huge upswept chevron. She could almost touch him as he hangs above her, grinning. His face changes: he is thinking now, concentrating. The downstroke of the wings begins slowly and gathers momentum as he forces his feet downward in the pedals and the hum of the pulleys becomes a whine. She feels the turbulent air bearing down upon her. Dust and debris blast away across the floor in the descending gale and the whole swaying contraption surges vertically upward into the dark vault. The wingtips droop for a frozen moment, downswept, mantling her in black shadow, and begin to rise again. The great traceried canopy of silk drifts upward toward the horizontal, locks with a click, settles back, swaying, into its moorings, and is still.

As he disentangles himself from the harness at the top of the teetering stepladder he almost falls and she laughs out loud. He descends to ground level, indignant.

"I could have broken my leg, split my skull. What's so funny?"

She holds him to her, strokes the petulance from his face. Her laughter is full of tears. He puts his arms round her and his hands drift inevitably to cup her buttocks. Sentiment passes over into lust.

He is kneeling between her outspread thighs as she sprawls on the piled clutter in the lamplit gloom, still inside her, but spent and shrinking away. His knees are cold. She holds his head to her breast. The long moment of ordinariness is too precious to forsake and they cling on to one another in the draughty echoing space, growing cold and stiff, holding off the time.

At last, they move. He walks her to the door and they stand together for a moment. Dawn is beginning to break and the morning star hangs in the pearly band of day which streaks the horizon. Talos, the King's giant is standing at the edge of the harbour, lizard still, his brass limbs edged with dawnlight. She looks at Daedalus but he shakes his head, kisses her as a sign that she should go. He watches her as she threads her way through the timber stacks until she is lost to sight. He walks over to where Talos stands at the edge of the dock. The giant's reflection wavers in the black water. Mirrored lights glimmer where the brass is polished from long use. An elbow, a row of knuckles, glint in the water. Daedalus sees himself in the water next to the great brass man, as if he were a small child, barely half his height. The dawn star dances in the black mirror above the giant's impassive features. The deepset eyes are lost, except for a tiny light in the depths. Talos blinks slowly and the tiny light is extinguished and rekindled. In the silence Daedalus catches the faint click-click of the metal eyelids. A dog barks somewhere.

They stand together as the sky gathers toward daylight. High up, gulls drift in the first unearthly rays of the unrisen sun. The cloud that stretches from horizon to horizon evolves from black to grey to crimson. The sun rises like a glowing coal, blood-red, shimmering as if it were seen through a fire and the turning waves of the sea curl in the lucent dawn.

Daedalus guesses that they are companions now, Talos and he, that the giant has been sent as a sign and that he will stay until the end. The magician is not afraid yet. The giant seems not to dwell under the sign of fear but under the sign of what is already written. Whatever befalls in his orbit has always been known, is merely the acting out of what was always waiting and Daedalus sifts the obscurity of his own thought for the comfort that might lie in it.

Each year he has seen the giant stand in the heart of the midwinter bonfire with his feet and legs glowing red in the roaring heat. He has watched him pass through the port on his long walk around the bounds of Minos' island each Spring, garlanded with flowers, waved at and wondered at in every town and village. Tiny children are held aloft to watch Minos' giant and old people are content to watch him pass, for Talos has always been the King's giant. He was the brass giant in the days when Asterius was the Minos and he walks still in these days of the crookleg king who killed the old man and drove out his brother to get his own arse on the throne. He has walked the coast of the island in the Spring and stood in the winter fires for as long as anyone can remember. Stories tell how he sank pirate ships off the coast by throwing rocks from the clifftops, and how he confounded the king's enemies by heating himself in the fire until his limbs glowed red and falling upon them, but no one living remembers such things.

His brass limbs are pitted and scarred with age, blackened from the fires, worn to a sheen at elbow and knee and knuckle. There is a green patina in all the creases of his face and in the scars and crevices of this body. The stillness in him echoes like a well. His is the silence under the silence. The mystery of his being is absolute.

Like everyone else in the world, Daedalus has known the story of Talos the Cretan giant since he was a child, and it seems to him that he has always known about the stopper in his heel and he knows that if the stopper is withdrawn, the ichor will drain out of the giant's body and he will die. It exists. He sees it now, sees something, as he glances down to the great blackened and scarred heel, a sort of flanged bolt head, just below the point where the hawser tendons of the calf muscle come together. It is the thickness of Daedalus' wrist, a little less maybe, and sticks out about the width of his index finger.

Already and unawares, a picture of the tool which could extract that flanged bolt has formed in the magician's head. It is a lever, an iron lever, a wrecking bar, curved in a half circle at one end. The end is flattened to a claw whose precise size and shape has already been computed in that flickering domain below his thought. What passes in his thought is that the stopper exists. It is there for him to see, has always been there for anyone to see. Why does Talos exist when all the world has always known his mortal secret? If what can be done must be done, must already have been done, why does the giant still move and live? Why has the world's mischief not already been wrought upon him long ago? Has he been kept in trust through all the years? Daedalus endures a flickering moment in which the life of the giant seems infinitely precious, vulnerable beyond bearing.

Yet he finds that he has left the giant's side and returned to his workshop. He has kindled a fire among the dead coals of his forge. He blows the charcoal to white heat. From beneath its sacking he hefts a bar of that iron which is still all but unknown in the world. The strange red rust comes away on his palms. The iron ingot is heavy with a terrible ambivalence, with possibilities for good and ill. He has seen an iron sword cleave a bronze weapon as if it were butter. Long ago and in another place he has wandered a broken landscape of tall furnaces where smelters laboured naked as devils to bring to birth the black iron from the red earth, intoning words of propitiation as they worked the roaring furnaces.

He thrusts the iron into the hottest part of the fire. Its colour passes from grey to red to shimmering orange as he turns it in the heat. He beats out on the anvil of his instinct the giant's bane. The tocsin ring of the hammer can be heard far away in the still morning.

Out by the harbourlight a bleary watchman yawns and stretches, catches the faint sound across the water, mistaking it for a funeral bell.

When the work is done Daedalus stands with one eye closed, turning the curved lever with its claw, watching for its truth. He knows that he has made what should not have been made, that it should be destroyed, heated up again and beaten back into oblivion, ignorance, brute and unformed substance. It seems to him that he has made the key to a door. Something in him wonders if Minos has sent Talos as a ruse, a stratagem, wonders if the fatal trick has just been played upon him. Has the crooked king destroyed him? Has he placed Talos in his path so that he will wreak that mischief upon the ancient giant which has lain in wait for so long? Daedalus is repelled by his own lying thought, shakes his head as he might to rid himself of a wasp, to rid himself of the shame for the act he has not yet committed, which he knows is his alone.

Even as he shakes his head in that private gesture of abnegation, his hand plunges the fatal engine into the quenching water. A simple act, unthought, unwilled, true.

31

"You're a liar."

"I swear, as Zeus is my judge."

"Off a cliff? You should go to Almiros. They're all liars there."

"Listen. It's the truth. I swear."

"Go on then. Start again. Start from the beginning, but get me another drink first."

The bar is solid with sailors and fishermen. The noise of their voices is a wall.

"Mind your backs. Here. Look out. Don't spill it."

"Cheers. Go on then, get on with your lie. Your dad an Almiros man, was he?"

"You know Sinon."

"Him with the limp, skipper of the Persephone?"

"A week ago, he come up to me. 'A day's work, up the coast,' he says, 'should be back before dark' 'Where we going?' I says. 'Lasithi.' 'There's nothing at Lasithi,' I says. 'Do you want the work or don't you?' he says, 'I'm short handed. I've got somebody sick.' So that was it. Beggars can't be choosers, and you know as well as me that things have been thin since all them boats was lost in that big wave last Autumn.

We left at daybreak, me, Sinon and that broad backed youth that never speaks. Nice enough day. Breeze from the south-east. Nice boat too, sweet as a nut. We come under the cliffs at Lasithi about noon and there wasn't nothing there. Why should I worry. I'm getting paid. And then we sees this smoke coming off the cliff top. Someone had lit a fire. We stood out from the cliff a few hundred yards and put out the sea anchor, and then this bird comes off the cliff. I shit myself. Biggest bird you ever saw. Its shadow covered the boat. I was shaking. I'd never seen anything that big before. And then it went up. It went up and up until you couldn't hardly see it. Like when you see an eagle in the mountains. You're not sure if you can see it or not.

And that boy, the mute, he wasn't frightened at all. He was laughing and capering about and pointing at it. And then you could see it again, circling down in great spirals like a vulture. It came down a long way and then it flew out to sea. Great slow wingbeats. But then it turned and started to come back and I thought, my god, it's got something in its claws. It's got a man in its claws. It was like a dream. I couldn't believe what I was looking at. It came closer and closer. It was huge, and it wasn't a bird at all. The bloke hanging underneath was working rigging and pedals. He was making it fly. It came up alongside where we was, about thirty yards off and about the height of the mast, and it hovered for a minute, like a great albatross. The man, he was shouting to Sinon and Sinon was shouting and nodding and waving his arms and it didn't mean nothing to me. And then it just sort of sank. The whole thing just settled down onto the water with the bloke underneath it. Sinon had this block and tackle set up at the mast head. I'd noticed it earlier on. He jumped over the side quick as a flash with the rope from the pulley block in his hand and swam across to where it was floating and tied on to it. We hauled on the other end, me and the mute. We pulled it clear out of the water. The bloke was half drowned and half frozen. He stood there with a blanket wrapped round him and his teeth chattering. He showed us how to fold the wings together just as if it was a great butterfly and then we made it fast to the boom. They weren't hardly made of nothing, those wings, thin spars no thicker than two fingers with flimsy cloth stretched over them, bits of stitching. Like a dragonflies wings, but huge, fucking huge.

On the way back Sinon, he said to me, he said, 'you haven't seen none of this, have you?' And I said, 'No, boss.'"

"What part of Almiros did you say you come from?"

32

Spring. In the sunlit lanes children crouch, tying coloured threads to butterflies. The insects rise unsteadily into the air, trailing their long streamers while the children pursue them, shrieking, and it would be a different world if they did not catch the ends of the threads so that the butterflies labour impossibly, failing, sinking little by little until they come to rest again in the country of their enemies. Perhaps one butterfly rises above the childish hands, rises into the pale spring sunshine trailing its gaudy banner. Perhaps.

There is still snow on the distant summits but the hillsides above the town are carpeted with the blue and purple vetch. In the evening when the breeze turns and blows off the land, comes the smell of lavender. By the harbour wall the strange horned poppies dance.

To the Northwest a pillar of cloud rises from the horizon. It is the smokes from the volcano on the ruined island of Thera. It sleeps no longer, though there is yet no other sign of its wakefulness save the rising smoke and the faint, deep furnace roar. The dark column ascends through banks of fleecy cloud, rising beyond sight. The traders in the temple who sell the little clay limbs, the arms and legs, ears, heads, feet, which the sick take into the temple and hang near the altars, have added a little volcano to their wares. It sells well.

Galleys come and go in the brisk spring weather, sails slapping as they heel into the foamcapped waves. Naucrate sits alone in the steep fields above the town amid the swooping flowers, watching the white wakes of the ships as they plough the bluegreen sea below. It is a Spring like any other. It is all life, renewal, becoming. She twirls a tiny frond of the purple vetch between her fingers and knows that it is not so. Beyond the blue Spring looms purple Summer, grapedark, stormy, riven by the lightning. She gets up, smoothing down her skirts, holding them out for a moment from her bare legs, letting the breeze play over her body, before she sets off down to the shipyard.

Talos is standing by the harbour wall, unmoving, eyes on the horizon, as she passes into the workshop.

Overhead, two sets of dragons' wings hang high up in the gloom. Below, Daedalus is mending a child's toy, a doll. He looks up as she enters.

"Does he come every day now, the King's giant?"

"Most days. He comes more often now, stays longer. He will act soon, I think."

"Act?"

"I don't know. I think Minos has sent him to prevent my leaving."

"Does he come in here?"

"He came in once and just stood for a couple of hours and then left. He had to crawl through the door on all fours. The refugees from Gournia left the next day. A bit disconcerting, I should think, a giant creeping in like that. It must have been bad enough with him hanging about on the quayside. They're living in one of the abandoned houses near the edge of the town. I think they were going to move out anyway. I've been to see them. They're digging the garden, planting things, as well as fishing. They don't mention Talos."

"What will he do?"

"Who knows. Destroy the wings, take me back to Cnossus, I don't know."

"What will you do?"

"Stop him, if I can."

"Can you?"

"Yes... I think."

There is a pause. She watches the broken doll in his hands. His hands are full of wisdom but he sits blankly, knowing nothing of himself. At last, Naucrate speaks.

"I am leaving here. Pasiphae has sent word. Her time is getting near. I shall stay at the palace for a while."

He turns the doll in his hands, thinking about what she has said.

"And after?"

"What kind of after can you imagine, Daedalus?"

He turns the doll in his hands.

"Will you send me a message, when her time is close?"

She moves across to stand behind him as he sits. She massages the tendons in his shoulders. His eyes close and his head drops forward slowly as she works and he speaks with his head bowed.

"I can only stop Talos by killing him. I think I would rather die. Maybe that's what will happen. As you say, I am not as clever as I think. It might be better. He is so... old."

"Leave. There is nothing you have to do. Leave. Spare him. You can choose."

"I do not know how to choose. I only know how to act."

She moves away, angry, pauses for a moment as if she would say more but changes her mind. He watches her walk away down the long workshop, catches the flicker against the light as she passes out of the sunlit door.

33

The mosaic floor of the colonnade is striped with warm sunshine and she walks in and out of the shadows. The earth-quake seems hardly to have touched this part of the palace; a cracked wall, a scatter of plaster. When she reaches the corner she turns and enters the spacious silence of the queen's apartment. The broad room with its coffered ceiling smells of cedarwood and the white marble floor is cool beneath her bare feet. Pasiphae is standing by high windows, a silhouette looking out, holding a long gown against her body. The winter shutters have been taken away and the wide landscape beyond the room is a great bright picture. Close at hand, trees toss new leaves with a sound like shingle in the sea's edge. Cloudshadows move over distant hillsides. The snow has gone from the mountains.

The queen turns away from the light and squints into the half dark of the apartment with that selfsame expression of puzzlement. It is an expression full of girlish uncertainty, candid, without anxiety. At last the queen makes out the fisherman's wife and she smiles, holding out her hands. Naucrate goes to her, takes the hands in her own.

"See me. See what I have become."

Pasiphae unfastens her gown and lets it fall to the floor, stands naked, big bellied, her arms outstretched, moving her weight from hip to hip in a wry parody of the movements of a dancer. She puts her hands on the taught shiny flesh of her domed belly, caresses it with a languorous motion. Her navel has inverted and sticks out. It is the omphalos, the world's navel. Her breasts are heavy, full, the brown aureoles of her nipples wide and dark. As Naucrate's fingers begin to move tentatively over the queen's skin, the teats stiffen, grow long and the nipple puckers. The hands sweep over the pregnant belly, into the small of the back, across the buttocks, down the rounded thighs. Naucrate kneels. The flesh has healed where the bull's horn has pierced it but the scar is deep and cruel, a livid crater in the smooth forward sweep of the thigh. The blue black snake is beheaded. She holds the thigh in her two hands and presses her mouth to the wounded flesh. Two women, figures against the great rectangle of light, a play, a tableau, the acting out of the real.

The queen takes her hand, "Here, feel, feel." and presses her palm against the taught flesh of her stomach. The stranger moves beneath Naucrate's palm in that first darkness, restless, knuckled, blind, yearning. She feels something else too, beneath her hand, something at the edge of the senses, hardly there, an echo: loss, despair. She speaks with an automatic and countervailing blandness.

"You are still carrying it high."

"Do you think it sees the light through my flesh?"

"The light it sees will be the colour of your blood."

"He wakes, you know, and sleeps. I can tell. Mostly he wakes."

Pasiphae rolls her eyes drolly and laughs. The careless laughter brings the prickle of tears to the eyes of the fisherman's wife.

34

Talos the giant takes to coming into the workshop, his great bulk blotting out the light as he creeps on all fours through the door. He stands motionless in the shadows through whole days and nights, whenever Daedalus is working. Sometimes Daedalus talks to him as he works, talks to the pale unspeaking eyes in the darkness.

It is late. Daedalus leans wearily against a bench, wiping the sweat from his eyes with a rag. He looks across into the darkness.

"My nephew was called Talos too. Did you know that? He is dead now. A long time ago. A clever boy, quick and sly, his mother's son. She sent him to work for me when he was twelve. I worked in Athens then. I had a workshop on the slopes below the citadel among the little blue and white houses.

I worked in bronze a lot in those days. I still think of myself as a smith. A strange trade. In the villages in the mountains they still hold metal working to be a branch of magic and the smiths recite spells as they work. I do it myself."

Daedalus wipes the grime from his hands.

"Do you already know these things, Talos? What do you know? Everything?"

He looks into the great impassive face. He cannot know what lies behind the pale unblinking eyes.

"Am I talking to myself?"

Is there the faintest slow shake of that massive brass head, the gravest ghost of a smile? He does not know. He bends again to his work. After a while he takes up his tale again.

"It is still a caste thing in those villages, metal working, handed on from father to son. They are like outcasts. They bury the dead. There is an old wives' tale which says that a pregnant woman should not go near a smith in case the child is born deformed. The boy children are still lamed at birth. I've never understood why they do that, cut the hamstring of the left leg. To stop them leaving? Stop them taking away the knowledge? Hephaistos is pictured as a cripple. I wasn't brought up to be a smith. My feet are still intact, though my ankle is bad.

Talos, my nephew was quick to understand things, but a fool just the same. He had a passion for casting objects into bronze. It is a simple enough thing to make a mould from a shell or a bone or a flower and then to pour in the molten metal. The results are sometimes striking. He once cast a fish spine in bronze. He did it badly so that the ends broke off. He sharpened the broken ends on a grindstone and told his mother that he had just invented the saw, even though saws have been in use for centuries in Athens, everywhere, but she, being a princess of the blood, knew no better. He told her that he had invented the compass too, and the potter's wheel, and she believed that too.

She had a dark passion for him. Now, at the Athenian court it is not a particularly uncommon thing for a mother to bed her own son, but this was different. There was madness in it. She was mad for him and he for her. They circled one another. She was my sister, well my half sister, we share the same mother. When Talos her son died, she said I had killed him, and in a way I did.

We were working on the citadel in Athens, Talos and I, on the roof of the temple of Athene, installing finials on the gable. Bronze emblems they were, as high as a man, covered in gold leaf. We'd been months casting them and now we were installing them on the top of the temple facade, setting them with molten lead into sockets let into the masonry. The temple stands in the west corner of the citadel where the cliffs fall sheer away below. From the temple roof you could see over the whole city and the plain to the sea. At dusk you could watch as the lights of the city were lit. Torches burned along the principal thoroughfares and you could mark the progress of the lamplighters as they made their way from one torchbracket to the next, like lines of fireflies winking into life. The lamps in the houses stretched away into the flat darkness, a great sea of tiny lights. Coals in the hearths glowed orange or red like planets. The sound of voices sometimes came up from far below, faint fragments of unknown lives.

Once or twice when we were doing that job and the scaffolding was on the temple front I went up there late at night with a flagon of wine to sit astride the great stone tiles of the roof ridge. It was summertime and the smells of the city came up in warm gusts from the darkness. It was as if the city were a lake reflecting back the stars. I had a woman up there too, sitting astride those tiles, looking out over that starlit sea. She was very beautiful, pale skin that glimmered white and hair black like the shadow cast by the moon. She had been brought as a slave from the far north by Phoenicians and had done her time in the brothels on the coast. When I knew her she was selling leeches in the market. I wanted to keep her safe, she was so beautiful, but that was just my vanity. She was not my creature, nor was my life her life. I had a passion for her, just the same. You know, I used to think that time not spent touching her body was time wasted. I couldn't keep away from her.

Talos died in the mid morning. We were hauling up one of the finials to the roof. It was in the shape of a serpent twined around a lightning bolt, bronze, as high as a man and as heavy as a bull. The gold leaf blazed in the sun as the finial turned on the end of the rope, inching its way toward the roof. Way, way below, you could see the crowds along the lane which ran around the foot of the cliff, craning up to watch the dazzling ascent of the sun reflecting gold. Sailors out on the sea caught the tiny flash, flash, as the heavy gilt bronze turned on the end of its hawser.

Talos was by the pulley wheel, high up, leaning out, shouting instructions to the slave teams hauling on the cable below, in his shrill, boyish voice. I could see him above me among the scaffolding, silhouetted against the blue cloudless sky. I saw the pole he was hanging onto break, saw him arc like a diver into the void.

There was no reason for him to have been up there in the first place, no reason for him to hang out like that, vain, stupid, shouting instructions to the slave teams who already knew their work, but then he was a boy, a prince brought up in all the exultant pride that goes with being a prince of the royal house, the world's greatest inventor, the sole and total passion of his own mother. What else was there for him but to die? He hit the steep slope below the cliffs with a cry, skidded and bounced down on his back, his limbs going this way and that like a broken doll.

I slid down the rope to the temple steps and then went over the parapet of the citadel on the masons' hoist to the slopes below the cliff. They were gathered around him when I came to where he was. He lay on his back. He had come down the cruel slope on his back. His eyeballs were shot forward in his head, and his teeth too, but he was still alive, breathing in and out in great rattling sobs. I took off my mason's apron, which is made of sacking and stuffed it in his mouth. I pinched his bloody nostrils between my fingers. I held him like that until he died in a great shaking of his broken body. I heard a voice ask what I was doing and I said,

"I am putting the snake in the sack."

It is the sort of thing that is said in dreams. What did it mean? It makes no sense, even to me. I didn't even know that that is what I did say until someone told me later. But, you know it's odd. At that time in Athens you could get a small reward from the city council for catching snakes on the slopes of the citadel. People out walking claimed to have been bitten by snakes. The town boys used to catch them out in the countryside and collect the reward anyway, pretending they had been caught among the citadel rocks. It became part of the town's folklore that the acropolis was infested with snakes. But the other thing is that Talos was of the house of Erechtheus, the house of the snake.

The words I spoke, "I am putting the snake in the sack." became a kind of saying. I hear it sometimes, even here. Sailors from the mainland still use the expression. It means, well, I think it means, I'm doing what has to be done, doing what is necessary.

When Polycaste, my sister, heard of her son's death and she heard what I'd said and done, she convinced herself that I'd pushed him from the temple roof. I was jealous, she said, of his superior gifts. I was taken before the city tribunal. The tribunal assembles on a bare rock, the Aeropagus, that stands below the citadel, overlooking the market. It is a plateau of white limestone, pocked with ancient post holes and there are steps cut so that you can climb up easily to the flat space at the summit. It is an open place, a good place, you might think, for justice to be meted out. It stands high above the market place. Away to the right was the temple of Athene and below it the steep cliff of the citadel down which my nephew had fallen. But knaves had been hired to lie. They said they saw me push Talos from the scaffold. Maybe that's what they thought they saw. I pointed out that only a fool would commit murder whilst being watched by hundreds of spectators. Polycaste, my sister, seemed not to recognise me. They banished me. It seemed like madness to me. There must have been things I didn't know, still don't know.

I took Icarus, my son, with me when I left. He was three years old, and he had not yet learned to speak and I knew that he would never speak. He was a quick child in many ways but vulnerable, fragile in his mind. I was afraid for him, afraid of what Polycaste might do if I left him in Athens. What she did, what my sister did, was different. I did not expect it. She hanged herself.

We went north into Attica for a while, and I did work in cities which owed no allegiance to Athens and then, after a couple of years, we came here. The story of how I killed Talos my nephew by pushing him from the acropolis is still told. I have sat and listened to a drunken sailor tell it in a bar on the waterfront. It seems that the soul of Talos took the shape of a partridge when he died, and flew away. I must have missed that bit."

Daedalus has stopped working. He sits vacantly with the hammer hanging from his hands, whilst in the shadows the eyes of the king's giant blink with a faint sound.

"I used to dream about it. For a long time I had dreams of Talos falling, but each time, in my dream, when I got to his broken body on the slopes below the cliff, it was not Talos at all. It was Icarus, my son."

35

It is late. The forge is lit, has been burning all day and through the night. From time to time Daedalus works the great bellows so that the sparks flow upward into the darkness and the charcoal is driven to incandescence, filling the place with weird light. Talos glints whitely where he stands by the wall, watching. High overhead hang the completed sets of wings like two dim dragons. This morning the magician woke from sleep, from the dream that he dreams each night now since he flew from the cliff, in the perfect knowledge that certain of the lashed joints in the wings will part, will fail to withstand the fierce demands of the wind unless they are strengthened. From bronze wire he is forging delicate pieces to reinforce those joints, trading off weight for strength as far as he dare. Those that are complete are laid out in rows on a bench nearby, ready to be fixed in place.

He is grimy and tired. The rims of his eyes are red. He fishes out a glowing fragment of metal from the bed of the forge with the heavy tongs and holds it against the anvil, shaping it with the hammer. The silence rings with the sound. He walks away to a lamplit space where the plans of the wings are nailed to a bench top, and pores over them, still holding the piece of bronze in the tongs. He walks back to the furnace.

Talos the giant has moved. He is no longer standing in the shadows by the wall. He is kneeling by the glowing forge with the knuckles of his hand resting in the white heat, in the space where Daedalus needs to return the metal. The magician looks up into the swimming quicksilver eyes.

"Talos, you are in my way. This is my work and you are in my way."

The knuckles of the huge brass hand are turning to dull red as they rest in the flames, are beginning to waver and glow. The fingers plough the burning coals, lifting a handful clear and letting them fall.

"Talos, this is my work."

The brass hand scythes across the coals, driving a spray of fire across the workshop. A rain of burning coals skitters and bounces across the floor. Daedalus dodges clear. The pale eyes are fixed on the man as he stands a few yards off. The great body climbs slowly to its feet with a sound like heavy ingots being dragged across flagstones, rises to its full height. The giant's head comes up against the bellows which hang over the forge from ropes. With a slight dismissive movement he pulls the bellows downward, snapping the ropes, so that they crash to the floor. Daedalus waits for the destruction to begin in earnest but there is a pause as the giant looks down to the ruined bellows at his feet. Nearby, a workbench is catching fire from the coals burning beneath it.

For a long moment nothing happens in that smoking place except for the licking of the flames up the burning bench. At last Talos turns to go, walks slowly away into the ringing darkness. The magician catches the scrape and clang as he crawls out of the door.

36

"You must go. Of course you must go."

Oenone is kneading dough and there is flour in her hair. She is not sure that she means what she is saying. The beadseller is standing unhappily by the window. He says,

"We shall come back. Six months, a year maybe, and we shall come back. It is good to have a place to come back to."

"The boy is ready to go. There is a restlessness in him. He has the instincts of a merchant. Maybe he is like you, like you were when you were his age. But he is still young, inexperienced. It is better that you go with him, this time at least. Now that the spring is here ships are leaving every day. It is a good time to go."

"I shall take him to Egypt, to the villages where the glass beads are made. We can buy merchandise there. The best beads in the world are made in those villages. Except for the ones made in my father's village."

She gives him an old fashioned look as she wipes her brow with her forearm, depositing more flour on her nose. He sighs, half absorbed in recollections of a distant childhood.

"And then we shall come back again. He can sell his beads around the towns of the island. And I can stand by this window again, or sit on the step in the sunshine, eat your bread."

He looks out of the window, affecting to watch the swifts whirling around the rooftops, which he only knows are there because of their screaming cries. He is trying to compose the right words.

"You know, for the first time in my life I have found a place that I do not wish to leave. This house. It seems to me now that I have been searching for this house for a long time. Does that sound foolish? And now I am afraid that if I leave it I shall not find it again. My eyesight is not what it was. I might miss it."

Oenone has stopped working. Her hands hang by her sides. Her fierce beaked profile is etched against the sunlit doorway and her wild white hair is full of daylight. She is vexed because, suddenly, despite herself, her eyes are brimming and she does not, will not, speak until she has control of herself. At last she says,

"You will not miss it. I shall put a light in the window."

37

Talos returns about noon. The bellows have been rehung and the forge is burning again. Daedalus is working once more on the bronze fastenings, though his stomach aches with suppressed fear and he is far gone in fatigue, so that the work goes badly.

There is a momentary sense of release in him as he catches in the tail of his eye the distant blink of light as the giant begins to enter the place. The time for uncertainty has passed. The magician drops his hammer and begins to work the bellows. The forge pants to a dazzling heat. He has guessed that as the giant walks toward the white light he will miss the wire which is stretched at knee height across the workshop. He does not know if the giant will see the wire. He does not know if the wire will snap. He does not know if the great ringbolts from which the wire is stretched will simply pull out of the masonry. And if the giant does trip and fall forward, he does not know if he will have the strength or the time to lever out the stopper from Talos' heel. He does not even know if the lever he has made will fit the stopper. He is a man in a dream, a man trapped inside a mountain, a man whose story has been set down long ago by strangers and never told to him.

The echoing dungeon tread sounds down the workshop, nearer and nearer. He stays as long as he dares, silhouetted against the fierce glow, drawing his fate toward him, then snatches up the iron lever and dodges sideways, out of the light. He runs half crouched back toward the approaching colossus and trips agonisingly over his own wire, sprawls, losing his grip on the lever, hears it skid across the paving stones into the darkness. Somewhere above him and to the side the massive shin drives forward into the wire. The magician lives through the rending of that instant in which all forces are balanced, feels the wire cry out as it goes bar tight, feels the mortar in the masonry begin its journey back to sand. Monstrous as a pine tree, vast, incalculable, the giant hangs over the abyss of his own destruction. Daedalus is on his hands and knees, sobbing and scrabbling about blindly for the lever. Talos begins to go down, topples away from the vertical. The great knee smashes a flagstone as it hits. The tower of brass goes over in a great grinding and thundering, an unfolding, engulfing cacophony, a layered, roaring requiem of toppling bells.

The magician's blind and bleeding hand finds the lever. Quick as a crab he has straddled the fallen hawsers of the giants calf, felt the black flanged head of the bolt with the raw ends of his fingers. The clawed lever finds its place with all the simple ease of the headsman's axe. He leans on the iron bar of his will. As unresisting and easy, as smooth and familiar as a recurring nightmare, the black stopper comes clear of the vent in a sudden gout of boiling mercury. Daedalus is an animal scrabbling clear of the scalding jet. The fountain pulses like a heart and the lake spreads outward in a slow tide of overlapping arcs, a smoking mirror in which the island of the dying giant is reflected. At its spreading margin fragments of debris on the floor catch fire as they are engulfed.

Talos is moving. He comes slowly to his knees in the spreading pools of his mortality. He climbs to his feet as if he were a diver at the bottom of the sea, ponderous, swaying, the open artery in his heel pumping out his life. His head moves from side to side. He is looking for Daedalus.

The magician is standing at the far edge of the smoking lake, on the dark bank of the Styx. The air has thickened, the giant is wading through the viscous pewter light toward him, swaying, phantasmal. Daedalus raises his head and looks into the giant's eyes and in that moment he endures another life, has a life thrust upon him, through him, dies another death. His chest is burst open by the great lance of Talos' dying. All is achieved, all understood, all forgiven.

Daedalus is only a moment away from his rest. He waits for that rest, avid for that silence. He is ready to be gone, has been ready a long time. Always, in all of his years, there was too much to be done and now everything is done, done with. He feels the shadow fall across him.

The great arms grope forward blindly. The huge man buckles to his knees and falls, and his fall is the ending of the world.

38

There is ash in the wind. As the morning advances the pillar of smoke which has hung on the horizon for weeks advances, spreads, becomes a lowering canopy, mantling the island, blotting out the spring skies. The light beneath this dark fulminating roof is unearthly and the deep, deep rumbling of the end of the world is heard again. Familiar dread returns. Outside the palace in Cnossus crowds gather, surging formlessly. Sensing jeopardy, the boy with the hare lip stays home and the crone who lives in the solitary cottage stays away from the window.

In the port, anxious labourers who have gathered in the shipyard nudge one another and point as the young woman passes through the timberstacks. Her face is cowled, her black cloak drawn close about her body. In the weird light she is a shade, a ghost slipping in and out of the sullen shadows. There is an urgency in her movements. She is not sure, in all this landscape of rotting hulls and mouldering warehouses, in this fearful noon, where the magician's workshop lies. She remembers a doorway without a door. She remembers waiting outside with the other women while the queen was inside the place, so long ago it seems. She looks about, aware of the eyes of the labourers following her. She seems to recognise a stretch of wall, the corner of a building, stonework scarred by the scraping passage of carts. This is the doorway. Is this the doorway? She steps inside, driven to escape the troubling gaze of the men.

It is dark, huge, echoing. She stands in the cavernous place, hearing the sound of her own heart. There is some strangeness in the dim light. Fleetingly she is filled with a memory of childhood. She is lying in bed in her grandmother's house in the mountains, looking at the ceiling and the ceiling is strangely light. It is the snow. Outside the window the land is covered in snow. It shines upward to the ceiling above the bed where she lies. She has never seen it before and thinks maybe she is still asleep and dreaming the lovely light. She stands at the window in her bare feet looking out at the strange white world. She goes back to the bed and lies down again so that she can look up again at the new lovely light on her grandmother's ceiling, wishing she could lie there forever in the strangeness of that light.

She takes a few steps forward. The whole floor is a mirror, a still, perfect surface, reflecting the light upward. In its depths, flawlessly reflected, she can see the distant vaults of the roof, a jagged lightning bolt of daylight where the masonry has cracked open to the sky. She can see dim dragons deep below the surface. She walks to the edge of the mirror and looks down at her own face staring up. Gently, she reaches out a foot to slide it across the mirror surface. It yields, trembling. The reflection of her startled face wavers.

Yards away, sitting on an island in the mirror lake is an incubus, a crouched and staring figure. It crouches, mad eyed, unmoving on the spine of the long brass island in the silver lake. Panic leaps into her throat, choking her. It is the queen's magician and he is watching her out of the glint of his eyes. She speaks, her voice reedy, whispery, unsteady.

"The queen wishes you to know that her time is close upon her."

"What? Louder. Louder. I cannot hear you."

"The queen's child is about to be born."

39

Naucrate stands by the high window which overlooks hills and valleys, watching the sulphurous canopy advance across the sky, watching the land grow dark as it passes into the sepulchre. She feels no surprise. A dusty wind agitates the trees and the leaves glitter for a moment in the dying light. She pulls the heavy drapes to, and turns back into the room.

Pasiphae is kneeling on the floor, naked, holding her great belly. Sweat beads her upper lip. Her eyes are closed and she pants with her mouth formed as if she were blowing candles out. She crouches, then stands up, clutching the bedcovers. The spasm ebbs, passes away, and the queen climbs wearily onto the bed and remains for a moment on all fours. She looks sideways at Naucrate from beneath a flag of hair and smiles a thin smile.

"How long does it take, do you think, to be delivered of a bull's child; for this is not the magician's child."

"I know."

"This one is altogether too restless, too strong, too angry. He thinks my womb is a prison."

She puts her head against the pillow and closes her eyes, murmuring.

"Asterion, I shall call him Asterion."

She falls into sleep as she speaks, still kneeling, with her backside in the air. Naucrate watches her face soften slowly into absence, grow vulnerable, girlish. After a while she persuades the sleeping queen onto her side and she does not wake. The fisherman's wife lies down beside her, against her back, and pulls the covers up and over them both. They lie like spoons. Naucrate has pulled up the front of her own dress so that they lie flesh to flesh.

She wakes in darkness and for a troubled moment at the edge of sleep she thinks it is her own contraction she feels. The queen is breathing hard as she climbs off the bed. She moves restlessly about the dark room, hanging on to the heavy drapes when the contraction grips her. One of her women enters with a lighted taper and moves silently about the apartment lighting the lamps in their brackets. The woman gives off anxiety, concern, like heat. Pasiphae catches her eye, gives her a wink and a smile. She returns to the bed and lies back among the pillows.

"I had a dream just then, when I was asleep. I am younger in my dream, a girl, still a priestess of the Mother, living in the sacred grove. It is a warm day. The sun is shining through the leaves of the trees and there is a breeze and the dappled shadows move about on the grass, troubling me. Nearby, I can see the river, and the sunlight is reflected off the moving water, so that I am dazzled and confused by the light. We are playing hide and seek among the trees and I can hear the voices of the other girls in the distance. I am standing with my back against a birch tree and I can feel the papery bark beneath my fingers. Someone is standing in the light but I am dazzled. I cannot see properly. It is a man. Somehow I know that the dazzling figure is a man. He moves toward me inside the light. He is tall. He has golden hair but I cannot see his face. He is coming very near. I can feel him close to my body. I feel the heat of his flesh. My thighs grow slack.

And then suddenly I am gone. The Mother has picked me up in her arms and carried me here across the sea. We look back together at the golden man and we see him as if he were in a tiny picture or a distant window. He is still standing before the birch tree but where I was standing there is a laurel bush. He looks puzzled. He begins to pull twigs and leaves from the laurel tree. He fashions a wreath and puts it on his head.

You know, if I were not otherwise engaged just now, I would go to one of Minos' soothsayers and tell him my dream and he would tell me what it meant, and then I would go to another and another, and they would all tell a different story. Men are fools, always arguing about what things mean. Everything is what it is."

Naucrate says,

"I dreamed I was having your contraction."

"You could dream you were having this one if you like. It would save me the trouble."

She closes her eyes tight and grimaces, showing her clenched teeth. She grips Naucrate's hand until the spasm passes. When it is over, they exchange looks.

"He is anxious to come, my bull child. Bring the women in. But first find me a comb, and a mirror. No. Hold me first. I am frightened."

40

Oily water slaps in the dark space between the ship and the dock wall. In the strange darkness a cold, blustery wind has risen and the sea beyond the harbour stretches away, unruly and rumpled, into the unnatural night. The timbers of the ship scrape against the stones of the dock as it strains at its moorings and the rigging chatters in the wind. They watch the baggage being taken aboard. It is dark at noon and the world could be ending and yet the labourers and the sailors go about their business in a dream of normality, like actors behind a darkened gauze. But crowds are gathering. Like the dead, they are drawn to the harbour and the dark water. The beadseller says to Oenone, with disarming understatement,

"We might have chosen a better day."

She laughs out loud and holds him to her in a gesture that begins in rough comradeship and ends in fierce affection. The boy seems not to notice the weird darkness nor the staring crowds. He watches the sailors as they make the ship ready for the sea. The boatswain shouts down to them from the height of the after deck and the boy tugs at the beadseller's sleeve. "Come. It is time. It is time for us to go." The old man understands, and for the briefest moment fear flickers in his expression. The boy tugs at his right sleeve and his left hand is in the old woman's strong grasp. He is nodding at her, and smiling through his blurred vision.

"Six months, a year."

"I shall keep the lamp lit."

The boy pulls him away toward the ship. She watches the old man follow him awkwardly as he clambers aboard. For a moment they are lost to view and then they appear again high up in the stern. The beadseller is hardly taller than the boy. He is looking for her but she knows that he will not see her because his eyesight is bad. She waves but still he does not see her. The big sail drops and cracks, balloons in the wind, and the ship is already gathering way.

Amid urgent shouting, the moorings are slipped and the ship heels, scraping noisily away from the dock wall and ploughing a curved, fluorescent wake across the dark, eerie waters of the harbour. She passes through the harbour mouth at speed and out into the dim, unruly sea with spray breaking over her bows. The old woman finds that she is running, pushing through the crowds. She runs around the broad top of the harbour wall, her black shawl flying behind her, until she arrives breathless by the stone lighthouse which looks out to the sea. The wind buffets her, blowing her white hair this way and that. For a moment she cannot see the ship, for it is already tiny, dwindling toward the horizon that divides the darkness and the darkness. She sees it, watches it flicker at the edge of sight and then it is lost and there is nothing at all to be seen on that wide unearthly sea.

41

The queen lies vacantly among the disordered bedding, at the centre of the anxious circle of her women. Her dark eyes are unfocussed and her lank hair is plastered wetly across her cheek. Her hands lie between her parted legs and her fingers caress the livid egg shape which is exposed between her thighs, the head of her child, which she cannot bring to birth. The head is too big. The wide bed is a sea of travail and pain in which, it seems to her, she has laboured all her life. In some remote place she understands that her flesh must tear if the child is to be born, but she will rest now, for a moment, just for a moment, and listen to the silence that is empty of the sound of her own screaming. Her heavy lidded gaze moves beyond the abject cluster of faces around her.

She sees the magician. He is standing against the far wall in the shadow, but she is slow to recognise him. She beckons him to her with a faint restless movement of her head. The women make a snakelike sussuration of clothing as he crosses the room. The queen's voice is a dry whisper and he leans close to listen to what she is saying. He catches the eye of the fisherman's wife who is sitting on the edge of the bed with Pasiphae's hand in her own. "This is too hard for me, magician." The voice is hardly to be heard. "But I am trying. He is almost here." She takes his hand and presses it between her thighs. Daedalus feels the knuckled cranium, hot, glabrous to the touch, feels her wet and cruelly stretched flesh.

The pain begins to rise up in her again and she clutches him, rocking forward in her agony, clinging on, crushing her moaning mouth against his shoulder. Her body clenches rigid and she bites off the scream that bursts out of her, sinking her teeth into his shoulder to the bone. The strength of her body gathers and is not to be denied. She thrashes beneath him, thrust out of consciousness by her body's extremity, her hands clawing at the child as it begins to tear free. Her scream is an inferno. As her flesh splits and the child is let into the world, she returns in that instant to herself, is there in the room, Pasiphae, the queen. She pushes Daedalus from her and curls forward to hold her child's emerging head and to watch as the baby begins to slide out on its tide of bloody fluid. She is trying to pick it up, to pull it toward her body but the limbs are greasy slick, ungraspable. The women stand motionless, locked in the monstrous moment. Naucrate picks the infant up and deposits it face down on the queen's belly and as she lifts it clear, the crimson afterbirth sluices noisily on to the sodden bedcovers. She pushes a towel between the queen's legs to stem the flow of blood from the torn flesh.

Pasiphae is barely there, sinking already toward exhausted sleep. Only half aware of what she is doing, she pulls the child up across her belly so that it can find the teat. The thick tongue searches, locks on to the nipple, sucks. She is gone, sunk into oblivion, her sleeping fingers straying over her child's head, caressing the nuzzling snout, the knuckled brow.

The fisherman's wife is tying off the cord. The women wake from their trance, suddenly aflutter with purpose. They pull away the bedcovers with their weight of butchers' yard mess and carry them out, returning with fresh bedding, water, whatever is needed, enclosing riotous creation within familiar routine.

When Naucrate has finished her tasks she looks about for Daedalus. He is standing by the wall in the shadows again and she walks over to him, wiping her hands on the hems of her bloody dress. He puts his hands flat against her abdomen, against the blood-soaked stuff of the dress, and she puts her own hands over his. There is blood under her fingernails. They stand together and there is no other place they can think of being than here, in this small place, in this moment. Across the room, the queen sleeps with her child at her breast. The circumscribed moment dilates. There is accomplishment, a resolution, rest.

At last he takes her hand and leads her out of the apartment. He walks a few yards down the corridor and turns into an empty storeroom. On the floor against the far wall is a bound box with handles. She recognises it. It is the box containing the model of the labyrinth beneath the palace. He takes off the lid. What she can see again is the palace without its roof, the warren of tiny rooms, corridors, antechambers, stairs.

"The labyrinth has several entrances. See there, the entrance marked with a blue dot. It is here, in this room."

He stands up and his hands trace the shape of a low door in the rough, limewashed wall. It has been painted over many times but she can see the hinges, the bolt. She has never noticed it before.

"You may have to lever it open and you may need to take a hammer to this bolt. It's years since it was used. If you are in fear of your lives, go down to the lowest level. Take the model with you. Use it like a map. Mark the walls as you go. There is a spring of water down there, good air from the caves below."

He looks down at her as she kneels by the box lifting away the upper layer so that she can see again the mazes of passageways in the layers beneath.

"Is this stupid? It may give you time, a safe place to be. I don't know."

She puts her hand on his arm. She sees in his face that he has killed the giant, and that his speech and his actions are coming out of an emptiness within him, like echoes. He has betrayed his nature, done both himself and the giant to death. He says,

"I must go. I am leaving. I am leaving with Icarus."

He turns to go but pauses in the doorway of the room with his back to her.

"You were right. I should have learned to choose. And now it is too late."

She listens to the sound of his footsteps receding into silence.

42

    The wind is coming off the sea, out of the dark horizon. On the clifftop it is blowing hard, making the sea grasses plunge and Daedalus is afraid that the turbulent gusts will bring them to ruin before they have started. He is buckling Icarus into the harness as he kneels beneath the outstretched wings and at every moment he is afraid that the plucking wind will find its way beneath the canopy and drag it to wreckage across the clifftop. The great wings buck and heave and Icarus is grinning fiercely as he resists the wind's buffet. His face is alive with exhilaration. Daedalus is checking agitatedly over the fastenings of the harness. "Stay near me, do you hear." he shouts above the wind.

    The boy is laughing in his joy as they kneel in the hissing grass, waiting for the lull, the lessening of the wind. They listen for the slack moment, clutching one another, and here it is, the little quietening in the wind's roar. Icarus stands up unsteadily beneath the swaying pinions while Daedalus hangs on to the straps of the harness. And then, with abrupt suddenness, he is gone, wrenched from his father's grasp, plucked up, whirled away by the renewed gust. The dragon man goes up into the sky with a great ululating cry. He rows upward into the gale, and there he is, tiny, exultant, crying like a falcon. The thing is achieved. The wind wimples the spread sails of silk as he turns and soars, drifts higher, circles.

    Daedalus stands a moment, craning into the sky, overcome, before he is submerged again in the fierce necessity of the moment. He creeps beneath his own wings as they lurch in the grass like something live. The harness, which he has made with his own hands, is a knot, a mare's nest, an unfathomable tangle. A gust lifts the wings and he is dragged in the eddy, even as he struggles to free the tangled straps, yards toward the edge of the cliff. He is fumbling like a man in a nightmare as the wings shift and drag across the ground. The wings lift again and he glimpses the void, the wrinkled sea crawling a mile below his knees. His feet search for the pedals in an ecstasy of fumbling as the whole apparatus loops upward in a sudden buffet and he is gone, over the cliff, planing steeply downward into nothing. In some mad, calm space in his mind he is listening to the frantic chatter of the silk and worrying that the whirlwind of his fall will split the fabric. His hand clutches among the controls and the dragon veers in its hurtling descent. His foot finds a pedal and he corkscrews inward toward the rushing cliff face. Seabirds explode from their ledges in raucous confusion. Another pedal. He is installed, but it is too late. The precise, lacy sea swell is rolling beneath his plummeting feet. He wrenches the dragon out of its dive with all the strength that imminent extinction lends him, oblivious to the rending shudder of pinions above his head. He is levelling out but his speed is terrific. His feet blast into the icy water in a blinding storm of spray. He is dragged, waist deep, gasping, and the wings slow, on the point of stalling, hang above the water, about to settle, and then the gust comes, lifts him away, up. He is gone.

He drives his feet into the pedals in pure, trembling relief, rowing the giant bird upward, rising up through screaming clouds of gulls, up past the lip of the cliff and the glimpse of sea grass, up toward the tiny, tilted, majestic circling of his son. They rise together like eagles, circling higher and higher until they are lost to sight.

They have passed into the dark cloudroof where the air is thick smoke, losing sight of one another in the acrid fog. They are flying blind, wings beating upward in the formless void. They emerge, as if rising from some phantasmal ocean, into a strange twilit zone where the air is clear. Below them, the fulminating smokes are a cauldron, a troubled sea stretching from horizon to horizon. High, high above, hangs another dark, vaulted canopy. There is no sun. It is as if they are flying inside some endless cavern. In the far distance, columns of smoke rise and fall like fountains, and there is a profound, abyssal sound of thunder. In the roped and folded architecture of these vast pillars of smoke, in their rising and falling, red fires coil, spilling a crimson brilliance through the halls of air. Red light bathes the spread wings as they labour.

Daedalus guesses that these vertical smokes are rising from the crater of Thera. The island volcano lies to the north-west and he changes his course so that they will pass to the left of these pillars of fire, taking a more northerly direction. High above, Icarus banks exuberantly to the left, following his example. Daedalus feels fatigue edging nearer, and hunger. He will eat necessity. His wings lift from time to time on a swell of warm wind that seems to be blowing toward the fiery columns. He turns more to the left, glancing upward to be sure that his son is aware of him.

His glance takes in the wings above his head for the hundredth time. He scans the complexities of the structure for asymmetry, failure, damage, and through the open door of that analytic instant pours, unbidden, aching disbelief, exultation, transcendence. He passes like a drowning man into some final lost place where thought is air, breath, where the space between thing and thing is abolished and the human heart is annihilated. He is flying in that last impossible dimension of himself that is neither flesh nor spirit. He is gone out into the world, riding its winds, a mirror.

The great sailwing lifts violently on a hot gust, tilts toward the fires, so that Daedalus is wrenched back into thought, must wrestle, wrest the wings back to mind. He comes to the simple and sudden realisation that they are caught in a wind that is spiralling in to the conflagration.

He begins to ascend. Above him Icarus keeps pace with his ascent, preserving the distance between them. Daedalus can think of nothing but to try to climb out above the danger, but all the time they are being drawn inward toward the towering ovens. The immense walls of oily, redlit smoke fill the world. Their tiny silhouettes rise slowly across the face of god, wingbeat upon slow wingbeat.

Burning fragments arrow upward out of the furnace, trailing white smokes as they fall away again. They are flying in a cathedral of rocketing and falling fire. Icarus is high above him, climbing upward through the tempest, growing smaller and smaller. Volleys of burning stones shriek upward. They whine past Daedalus like hornets.

Though he cannot see, he sees it. Icarus is hit. It is his dream. A burning stone crashes upward through the fragile tracery of the wings and the dragon wings lurch brokenly. He is hit again and the wings begin to distort, to come apart. Icarus is falling, tumbling over and over. He falls past Daedalus. He is reaching out. He passes so closely that his father can see his face, sees all his fear, his emptying out. Icarus has seen him, has reached out his hand toward him. He is falling away, dwindling, diminishing, growing tiny as he turns over and over. Fragments of the wings follow him, spiralling and fluttering, into the gulf.

The world empties out. There is nothing but the roaring of the void. Nothing remains but the undergoing. Daedalus rows upward and upward, knees driving down in a rhythm of agony, toiling like a galley slave. His chest is bursting. The crimson cauldron falls away below his feet. Above his head the sky is aching azure, darkening to indigo, to midnight.

He gives over, spent utterly, annihilated, hangs crucified in the harness as he drifts among dark stars. His limbs grow cold. His fingers extend, his bones become one with the lineaments of the dragon. He is the dragon.

CODA

CODA

1

The mountain is a white ruin, a city of quarries, whose faceted walls rise in jumbled ranks one above the other to the distant summit ridge. Steep roadways and ramps of broken stone zigzag across the eviscerated slopes. It seems an abandoned, inert landscape, until, in a certain breathless instant, the eye registers the seethe of human labour. In that moment in which the first microbial figure resolves into intelligibility, the scale of the termite war against the mountain blooms in the mind. A twenty ton block of stone, levered away from the vertical and crashing flat in a gale of white dust, is a detail lost in the vast crepitation. Bullock teams, thirty strong, are ants. They move and do not move on the long ramps. Everywhere on the white anthill slave teams labour.

There have always been quarries on the mountain. Its stone is always being, has always been, stolen, carted away along the straight road that arrows across the plain to the sea. There are white marble palaces and temples scattered across the world and white ruins on grassy plains where brigands make their fires, where once there was only the mountain.

In the morning, in the dawnlight before the sun begins to stain the sky, the smashed mountain is a blue silent fortress, a formless necropolis. At noon and through the afternoon it is all clanging white, and the eye aches for the lengthening shadow and a softening of the light. At last the westering sun grows huge, seems to hang too long, wavering like a fire, above the toothed precipices, and sinks. The fretted skyline grows black, precise, and the air softens to a tranquil and fogged violet. Veils of dust billow in the evening wind, spin in roaming vortices among the shadowed quarries.

It is almost night and the workteams have given over for the day. Bullocks munch in the crepuscular halfdark. Torches and cookfires glimmer here and there. High up, near the ridge, a cluster of torches burns, like a little constellation of stars. Someone is working late.

The high walls of this quarry glow in the torchlight like a stage set. A solitary stonecarver is working on a piece of stone, casting fantastical shadows. The tink tink of his hammer can be heard for miles through the still darkness. A woman stands at her door in a village out on the plain and hears the sound, tiny, exact. The stonecarver drives the claw chisel over the furrowed surfaces of the stone. Already the stone is a lion, huge, full of menace in that uncertain light. Stone muscles bunch in its haunch. It is twice the height of the man, a monster. He works from a scaffold of wooden poles. His head is shaved like a slave and his skin is caked in dust and sweat. Sinews run like ropes in his arms and shoulders as he works. There are two scars on his left shoulder, small semicircular marks, deep, as if he had been bitten by an animal.

He wakes from sleep in the red, silent dawn. His blanket is damp and pinpoints of red light reflect the risen sun in the beads of dew which cling to the weave. Near his face on the stone parapet, half eaten food and an empty wine flagon. Far below, across the shadowed cliff, a solitary rider dismounts and begins to lead his horse up a steep ramp.

The stonecarver is already at work when the king's messenger arrives in the quarry. The slaves eating at the long plank table in the level sun, glance up at the hollow eyed youth in his plastered finery. The overseer points to where the stonecarver is working. The young man stands below the scaffold.

"Excuse me, sir. I have a message for you."

He fidgets with the sealed letter. The stonecarver glances down.

"I have come from Camicus. I have a message from Cocalus, the king. He requests your presence."

2

The ship weathers the cape and beats, close hauled, into the brisk, sunlit bay. She is heavily laden with blocks of quarried marble and she wallows, with the rainbow spray breaking over the side. The city is a smudge of white on the coast. From his place in the stern by the steersman, the stonecarver watches the distant blur of the waterfront resolve imperceptibly into wharves and warehouses and forests of masts at the quays, as the ship plunges through the whitecaps towards the town. There are more ships anchored out in the bay, maybe thirty or forty of them. It is a foreign fleet, warships. The stonecarver is aware of the consternation around him. The eyes of the crew are everywhere as the steersman picks his way between the high, black-tarred galleys. Below the surface the bronze clad beaks bask like sharks at the bows and impassive faces stare down as they pass. The stench of galley slaves is a foetid corridor in the lee. They are Cretan warships. It is Minos' fleet. The stonecarver is in no doubt. Through the swaying vista of masts he glimpses the royal pennants and wonders if it is Minos himself. He listens to the nervous speculation of the crew. Their agitated voices have risen a pitch and there is false laughter as they pass into the shadow of the brooding galleys.

The mate brings them to with a curse and the rope's end. The ship emerges from between the anchored galleys, nearing the town. The long boom is lowered down the mast and the saltstiff folds of the ochre sail are gathered in. The ship loses way as she noses in toward the quays. The stonecarver can see the bottom through the clear water. He watches a giant turtle, ten feet down, row languidly into the shadow beneath the hull. The stone anchors fall in unison and the ship bridles, then begins to swing slowly round on her tether. The stonecarver watches the harbourmaster's skiff emerge through the jumble of shipping. He can see no sign of Cretan soldiery along the waterfront. The business of the town seems as usual. He picks up his bag as the skiff ties up alongside.

"Ah, good."

Cocalus' bald head comes up from his game of chess as the stonecarver enters. The king is tall, cadaverous. His age is impossible to guess. He looks sick but will live forever. He cultivates an enervated demeanour to confuse his enemies.

"Did you see what the sea washed into the bay? A courtesy visit, my arse. What do you suppose he wants, him and his ugly black ships and his hired pirates? The word is that a month ago he put in at Syros and burned the town, hanged Iolaus the king. But look. Come here. Look what he sent. What do you make of this?"

The stonecarver walks over. On a gilded tray is a shell, a chambered triton. It curves in a perfect spiral, delicate, paper thin, as if it held the secret of the world. Next to the shell on the tray is a coiled length of linen cord. The stonecarver picks up the shell and listens to the lost sound of the sea hissing in its fragile labyrinth. He turns the smooth curves under his palms. Near to the end, where the spiral winds to a point, a small hole has been drilled. He looks at Cocalus.

"A messenger came ashore with it days ago. What did the fellow say now?... 'Minos proposes a game. Thread the cord through the shell if you can. If you succeed he will exchange the threaded shell for your own weight in gold. He wishes you well and will await news of your success.' He's been out there for a week. What's he up to? I sent an envoy out to keep him quiet. Fraternal felicitations, that kind of thing. I ought to invite him ashore, throw a banquet for him. It's this business with the shell I can't fathom. Is it a game? Is he mad?"

The stonecarver gives him the ghost of a smile.

"Anyway, I want you to thread the wretched shell. I don't want to invite him here and look a fool. I've tried. I can't do it. Nobody in the court seems to have any ideas. I even went down to talk to the chamberlain to see if any of his people could think of anything. They tried using thread stiffened with wax. They tried wire. Everyone says it's impossible. Someone suggested cutting it open and sticking it back together, doing it that way, but that would be cheating, and anyway, think how demeaning it would be if he noticed. So that's why I sent for you. I thought I'd send him an invitation tomorrow, after you've had the time to thread the stupid thing."

The king drops the shell into the stonecarver's hands as if the matter were thereby solved. He drops the linen cord into the open end and dusts his hands together. The stonecarver's face is a blank. As he is leaving the chamber with the shell, Cocalus calls after him.

"I'm glad you're back. The girls have been like snakes since you left. They killed one of the slaves. Beat the poor creature to death, and then... they hung her up by the neck and stuck things into her eyes. It wasn't pleasant."

3

The stonecarver leaves the shell and the cord on the cot in his room and goes down to the harbour to scrounge another triton shell. The gossip on the waterfront is nervous, speculative. Glances stray to the dark ships in the bay. The Cretans have been ashore for water. Skiffs from the town have been out to the fleet selling fruit and shellfish. The whores are too frightened to try their luck. There is a feeling of something impending. Fortune tellers do well in the bars. There is heavy drinking, false laughter.

He asks the fishermen mending their nets where he will find a knifegrinder's shop and they direct him to the steep narrow street behind the slipway. The shop is a dark, cluttered tunnel of a place. A forest of dusty blades, scythes, swords, axes, pruning hooks, hangs from the ceiling. The knifegrinder has two circular grindstones mounted on kickwheels, the one somewhat finer grained than the other. The old man works the wheel while the stonecarver holds the shell he has bought against the spinning stone. He holds the side of the shell against the grindstone. The gritty white dust comes off in little clouds and the secret chambers of the spiral shell reveal themselves little by little. He continues until only half of the shell remains and he can see its secret perfection.

He sits in a bar with the shell on the table in front of him, drunk. He has been watching it for a long time, the shell. The solution is obvious, even though he is not sure it will work. Did he always know the answer? He is sure, in his cups, that all of the answers to all possible questions are already in the world and that the answers have merely been mislaid or forgotten. It is simply a matter of being still and listening, or rather, not listening. He also knows of dark places where there are neither questions nor answers. Some things are hidden and there are no questions to be asked of them, but it is a mistake to think they do not exist. He shepherds his drunken thought, guiding it away from the precipice. The bar is empty.

Outside in the darkness, thunder rumbles. He buys another flagon and leaves unsteadily, clutching the shell and the wine. The rain comes on heavily, raking the dark cobbles of the harbour. He finds a place on the beach beneath a boat, sheltered from the downpour. A hundred yards off on the water, jagged lightning splits, close enough for him to hear the hiss before the deafening thunderclap. Out in the bay, in the ships of Minos' fleet, thousands of men lie awake in darkness, listening to the fearsome detonations of the lightning and the sound of the rain on the sea, willing the storm to pass. Minos turns beneath the heavy coverlets, whimpering in his dream.

Dawn finds the stonecarver above the town, among the scattered pine trees, poking the stony earth with a stick, still clutching the shell and the remains of the wine. He moves up the hillside with his eyes down. The ground grows broken and the white limestone breaks through the earth like teeth through a gum. Tree roots clutch bare rock. He crouches. Between his feet foraging ants are manoeuvring the corpse of a spider across the white stone, through crumbs of soil and fallen pine needles. A few feet to his left, he is suddenly aware of an ant road. Insects move in both directions. He thinks of the armies of slaves on the quarried mountain. He thinks of the unfinished lion. He creeps along next to the ant road until he comes to the ant city. It is a mound, about half his height, made of soil and pine needles. Ant roads wind toward it from all directions. Using the shell he scoops into the side of the city.

Cocalus' daughters catch him as he carries his shell full of ants along the shadowed corridors of the palace, slipping out at either side and clutching his arms, murmuring, touching his face. The princesses are twins, stick-thin, feline, their ageless, parchment white faces haloed in wild frizz. Pulling and cajoling like goblins they usher him along the passages to their apartment.

It is a strange place, the princesses' apartment, though it seems less strange to him now than it did at first. The once luxurious suite of rooms is piled and festooned with unlikely rubbish. The curtains are drawn and the filtered light lends the place a troubling, deranged atmosphere. There are skeletal plants and flowers everywhere, long dead. Piled against the walls and scattered in drifts across the filthy marble floor, there are dozens, hundreds, of shapeless bundles wrapped in sacking and tied with string and rope. It is impossible to tell what they contain or how long they have been there. The stonecarver knows that some of them contain the bodies of cats. Beneath the fug of stale incense the place has the smell of an embalming house.

They lead him through to a dim space which has been cleared of debris. Sacking bundles are arranged in a circle to mark the edge of the area. At the centre, hanging from the coffered ceiling by its neck is a jointed wooden figure. Its head and limbs are stuck full of nails, which give it a swollen look, like a corpse. Other wooden figures sit around the circle, adorned with crowns and fantastical headgear, holding bundles in their laps. They lean against one another, heads bowed, stick fingers unmoving.

The women coax him down with little gestures to the place of honour, a filthy rug on the floor between two wooden figures, before entering the circle themselves. It is a play, a performance, dumb crambo. He watches them greet the company with elaborate courtesies. They light lamps around the base of the grisly totem, moving in a parody of temple ritual. They begin to dance, prancing in his direction like whores, hoisting their shifts, blue veined shanks akimbo, cunts spread between painted fingernails. They are children putting on a show. It is a greeting, a welcome. They are welcoming him back to their mad, lewd domain. Next to him, ants make their way over the lips of the shell.

In his room he tips out the contents of the half shell onto the wooden table and sifts through the debris and the milling insects. Near the edge of the table, weighted down by a pebble so that they will not waft away, are lengths of gossamer thin silk which he has teased out of a piece of fine gauze. Ants scurry in all directions. Licking thumb and forefinger he lifts an insect clear. It seems an impossible job. He lets the ant go and takes up a length of gossamer. He makes a tiny loop near the end. He nips another ant between thumb and finger and passes the loop over the back end of the insect.

As he tries to tighten the loop using his teeth and his free hand, the tiny creature escapes and drops to the table. He smears it into the wood in his irritation. He tries again, though his tongue is thick from drink and his head aches. This time he succeeds but when he lowers the tethered ant to the table it drags around in a circle. He holds it up on its thread close to his eye and sees that he has deprived it of two of its legs in the struggle. He smears it, cursing. Making himself breathe slowly, he tries a third time, his shoulders aching with frustration. This time it works and the ant fiddles the air heroically at the end of its thread against the great dark moon of his eye. He picks up the triton shell and lowers the ant down toward the drilled hole at the tip. The tiny creature clings on to the edge, refuses to enter the shell. He nudges it with his fingernail, again and again, and at last it disappears inside. The stonecarver breathes out. He scoops honey on his finger end from a jar he bought in the market and smears the outer rim of the shell, even though he isn't quite certain that ants can be attracted with honey. He deposits a fingerful of honey on the table among the milling ants, to make sure, and it disappears instantly beneath a hundred frantic insects. He watches the thread disappear little by little into the drilled hole and then it stops. He waits, poking extra thread through the hole, wondering if the weight of the thread is too great for the insect to drag. Nothing happens. He grows impatient, and is about to try a second ant, when the thread begins to move again, and stops again. He waits, it moves a little, it stops, he waits. His shoulders are rigid and the edges of his vision are black and wavering. He scrabbles under his cot for a bottle, extracts the cork with his teeth and takes a long pull, and then another. He waits, drinks, grows vacant watching the multitudes of ants milling around on the table in the debris of the nest. At last he picks up the drilled shell and peers absently into its open mouth. At the lip, the ant is feeding on the honey, its gossamer tether stretching back into the dark interior of the shell. He teases a length of thread through and snaps it off close to the insect. It wanders off across the table trailing its piece of silk behind it. He finds the linen cord and binds the gossamer thread around the end. Gently he pulls on the thread, easing the cord through the drilled hole as he does it. The linen cord emerges. The thing is done. He wipes away the honey from the shell's lip, ties the two free ends of the cord together and stands up, easing his aching shoulders. He falls face forward on to his cot and is instantly asleep.

In his dream there is a box. It is huge, bound with brass. It stands in a sandy underground place where torches burn smokily. He paces around the box, six paces along its length and two paces across. Six, two, six, two, around and around. Inside the box is a dead giant. This is what he does in his dream, walks around the coffin of the giant. But listen. There is a sound, a knocking. The giant is not dead. Listen. There is a banging from within the box. Listen! It is the giant. The giant is not dead! He is not dead! In his dream he is shouting and crying for joy. The sound of the knocking is like thunder.

He wakes. Outside his door, the king's page is rapping on the doorframe. The stonecarver stumbles to his feet, picks up the threaded shell and half opens the door. He pushes the shell into the youth's hands and returns to his bed. He falls back into his dream, going down like a drowning man. In his dream he is walking around the dead giant in his great box again.

4

Cocalus' palace stands above the town on a steep, rocky promontory, a tall fortress looking out over the jumbled rooftops and the bay. Beetling high above the harbour, balconies cling to its vertical ramparts of stone. There are awnings and banners, hanging motionless. The air is close, oppressive, expectant. There are no gulls swinging and crying across the face of these cliffs of masonry. They doze a hundred feet below on the oily water of the harbour. Yellow eyelids droop.

Cocalus sits with a blanket over his knees watching the horizon. Across from him, Minos sits, turning the threaded triton shell slowly in his hands, his fingers exploring its subtle surfaces, questing for subterfuge. His fingernail taps and the sound is pure, bell like. He draws the linen thread forward and back through the shell. He is avid for some sign that the shell has been tampered with but knows he will find none. His ruse has succeeded. Fear and exultation rise up within him.

"It would seem that you have succeeded, Cocalus. I congratulate you."

The old man makes a slight, self deprecating gesture.

"Iolaus, who was king in Syros, tried to cheat me, you know. He cut open the shell I had given him. He threaded the shell and stuck it back together. So stupid. I burned his city."

He smiles pleasantly. Cocalus is watching the sky darken as the squall advances out of the horizon. He looks across to where Minos sits with the shell and returns the smile, faintly, but says nothing.

"There are matters I must speak of, Cocalus."

Minos is staring into the shell as if it were a crystal ball.

"There is a demon who walks in the guise of a man, and I have been called upon to destroy him. I have been called. It has become my life's work. This demon in the shape of a man was a servant of mine. He posed as an inventor, a maker of things."

Minos' voice is unsteady, the tone false, wracked, held back.

"This demon brought down ruin and confusion upon my kingdom.

He summoned earthquakes and great waves. Whole cities slid into the sea. He killed the sacred bull with a thunderbolt and caused the queen to give birth to a monster. He killed my giant."

There are tears running down his cheeks.

"He did these things secretly, disguising his true nature. But at last I found him out. I looked through the eyes of the man into the eyes of the demon and confronted him. When he knew I had discovered his secret, he built great wings and flew away."

Minos struggles for a long moment to regain his composure.

"And I will be frank with you, Cocalus. There was a time when I was afraid to pursue this demon. I was afraid he would destroy me. But now I am ready. I have taken measures. I have prepared myself to wrestle with the demon. On my ship is a cage of iron. Do you know of iron? It is a black metal, adamantine, imperishable. I have caused chains and shackles of iron to be made. I have priests too, magicians and necromancers, skilled in the demonic arts. I have brought my torturers. I shall subdue my enemy at last."

The crippled king has reassured himself with the sound of his own voice. He leans forward, eager, fervid.

"I set a trap, you see, a trap to catch my demon. I baited a trap. This is my trap."

He holds the shell in both hands against his cheek.

"You see, my demon is cunning. He answers riddles, finds answers where there are none. Here, for instance..."

Minos pulls the linen thread slowly back and forth through the triton but his eyes are on the king.

"This game of the shell was a question with no answer, and yet here it is, the answer. I believe I have found my demon. What do you think, Cocalus? Have I found my demon? Have I found him?"

Cocalus is watching the incoming rain blotting out the rooftops of the town below. The first heavy drops make a sound on his blanket. The brocaded awning lifts in the first gust of wind, lifts again, flaps, chatters like a flag as the storm breaks over the palace. The rain comes on with a roar.

5

Cocalus paces his chamber, up and back. Beyond the window, out over the grapedark bay, thunder rolls. His step is firm. The round white eyes of the princesses follow him as he paces, clutching one another as they sit by the window. The stonecarver stands by the throne.

"Shall I take his gold? Shall I do that? Shall I load you with chains and hand you over to him? It would be expedient, sensible, profitable even. What do you think?"

The twins are on their feet, trembling in agitation. The stonecarver speaks slowly, as if unaccustomed to speech.

"I think you should kill him now, while he is in the palace, and then burn his fleet."

Cocalus looks at him and their eyes meet.

"That is what I was thinking. Who does this crookleg bastard think he is?"

The princesses have crossed the room in a sussuration of silk and laid sudden siege to their father. They catch at his clothes, stroke his face. He leans into the little storm of whispering and listens with his head slightly on one side, his expression attentive. At last he raises his eyes toward the stonecarver.

"My daughters say they want to kill Minos themselves, but they need your help. They have thought of a way, it seems."

They tug him along, holding a hand each, circuitously through the royal apartments, avoiding those chambers where Minos and his captains have been housed. They lead him up twisting flights of stairs and along corridors. They push open a heavy door and enter an unused room. It is empty save for broken and discarded furniture piled against the walls. Two butterflies dance in the dusty light. The wooden floor is bare. The madwomen leave him at the door and pace about the room with their eyes down. There is a flurry of whispers and they kneel, tracing along the joints between the floorboards with their fingernails. They carefully lift a section of wood away and beckon him over, signalling for him to be silent. He kneels and peers down. Directly below, in the chamber beneath, is a bath. Towels hang over its rim and into the water. The water steams slightly. As they kneel, heads together, looking down into the room below, Minos passes, naked.

6

"It will be a ticklish business. We can arrange for his bath to be prepared for him in the evening, before the banquet. Will he make a lot of noise?"

The stonecarver shrugs. It is the least of a hundred questions he does not know the answer to. He feels sick with something that is closer to horror than fear, and yet there is elation too, in what he feels. He has never planned the deaths of men before. They are on the razor's edge, he and this king.

Cocalus says,

"How many of the ships' captains did he bring ashore with him?"

"Nineteen. There are thirty eight ships in the bay."

"So that means that there are maybe twenty ships out there with a captain. We'll have to get rid of the nineteen at noon tomorrow when they eat. I'll take Minos into the vault for the afternoon. My trinkets will amuse him. I don't care what he sees, do I? What about the fleet? There must be three or four thousand men out there. I've only got a couple of hundred men here in the town. If we fail we're dead meat. Have you thought of a way?"

The stonecarver nods without conviction. He says,

"I shall need slaves who can swim, married ones, about eighty of them. I shall offer them their freedom in exchange for swimming out in the darkness to the fleet. Their families will remain in the barracks as hostages. Your men will need to organise the townsfolk to kill the survivors when they swim ashore. You'll have to put me in command. There isn't the time to argue."

"How will these slaves set fire to the ships?"

"I don't know yet."

"You don't know? This is tomorrow night we're talking about, and it's almost noon now."

"Something will come to me."

"I have led a quiet life, these last few years. Why am I doing this?"

7

The stonecarver is alight. He moves through the hours with an intensity that boils away from him like smoke. Cocalus takes him to the barracks and formally hands over the command of the garrison to him. Once the stonecarver has made it clear to the assembled troops that he intends to destroy the fleet they are kindled with his fire. It glitters in their eyes.

He sits for an hour with the officers. He lists the things that need to be done and the captain of the garrison allots men to the tasks as he sees fit, and sends them off, some to recruit those slaves and free men who are willing and able to swim, some to bring in cartloads of straw from the farms, some to requisition quantities of oil and sailcloth. The stonecarver sends out for sailmakers.

Only he and the captain of the garrison remain in the room. He is a good man, the captain, solid, trustworthy. He has come up through the ranks here in the palace. He has a family. He is a peacetime soldier. He has seen few corpses and created none. The stonecarver puts him into the furnace.

"Tomorrow at noon you must take as many men as you need, to the hall where the Cretan captains are eating, and you must kill them, all of them. There are nineteen of them. How you do it is up to you. None must escape. If word gets out to the fleet, it will be the town that burns tomorrow night, not the Cretan ships."

The captain of the garrison nods. His world has just ended. Nothing will be the same again.

"One more thing. Tomorrow night, the moon goes down about two hours after midnight. As it sets I want you to set fire to the houses on the hill behind the town."

The captain's eyes dilate in his square, impassive face, but he asks only,

"How many houses?"

"Five. Ten. As many as will divert the Cretan lookouts."

The stonecarver turns to go.

"Tomorrow night we shall attack the fleet from the open sea. If the lookouts on the ships are watching houses burn in the town they will be less likely to notice us swimming in from the sea."

He winces at the assurance in his own voice. Its power baffles him. The tissue of his plan is nothing, a precarious pile of possibilities. He might just as well spin coins. It does not exist until he speaks. His words are flames, stones.

As a sudden afterthought he sends a couple of men down to the harbour to talk to the boatmen who have been ferrying out water casks and selling fruit and vegetables each day to the ships of the fleet. It occurs to him that a bad case of the flux among the Cretans will serve his purpose well. One thing that saps the concentration is the shits.

He goes to the chamberlain and asks for two of his metal workers. He takes them up to the empty room above Minos' bath and explains what he wants done.

"Make what you need in the workshops. Don't make any noise up here until the afternoon. Have it finished before dusk."

It is almost midnight. The assembled swimmers stand about, dripping, in a yard between empty warehouses by the harbour, in the flicker of torches. The stonecarver has had them swimming up and back across the harbour for hours in the darkness. Several volunteers, willing, but unable to swim well enough, have been pulled spluttering from the water and sent away.

The stonecarver is standing next to a large sailcloth sack which has been stuffed with straw and stitched up tight. It lies there on the stones like the carcass of some slaughtered beast. A rope is tied around the middle of the sack. The rope has a long free end. Where the rope is tied around the sack, a weight is clamped, such as fishermen use to hold down their nets. The sack has been painted with a mixture of oil and soot. He looks around at the wide attentive circle. His voice is a door to the furnace.

"The ships of the Cretan fleet are black. You can see that for yourselves from the harbour. And the reason they are black is that the Cretans paint them with pitch to keep them watertight. Pitch burns. It burns very well."

His eyes move around the circle, fixing the listeners.

"This sack is full of oiled straw. It burns well too, and it floats well. Tomorrow night you will walk out to the headland at the point of the bay. You will be given a sack such as this, two men to each sack, and you will be rowed out to the seaward side of the fleet in fishing boats. When the moon goes down you will get into the water with your sacks and swim with them to the Cretan ships. When they are at anchor the Cretans lash the steering oar close alongside the ship so that the paddle of the oar is still in the water. Push the sack into the space between the steering oar and the ship and tie it in place with this free end of rope. Set fire to the sack and swim to the shore."

He looks around and catches the obvious question. He picks up an oil lamp from the floor. It is burning invisibly under a little clay cowl. He removes this hood so that the flame can be seen.

"When the sack goes into the water it will float with the fisherman's weight at the bottom. You will tie a lighted lamp like this to the top side. It cannot be seen under its hood. Even in the sea swell it should not go out. When you have attached the sack to the ship, use the lamp to set fire to it. Swim to the shore. Get ashore as quickly as you can. Later there will be Cretans swimming ashore and there will be people waiting on the beaches to kill them, so shout as you approach. It is important they know who you are. You can get your bearings from the lights of the town. There will be large fires on the hill above the town.

I want you back here at noon tomorrow. We shall walk out along the clifftops and work out who is to swim to which ship. There are only thirty eight ships out there. It should be possible. And then we shall come back to the harbour and you will practise with the sacks. There is no reason why any of you should die tomorrow night."

He tips the lighted lamp over onto the oiled sack of straw. Flames lick for a moment, catch, erupt into a wall of fire. It casts a lurid light on the circle of faces. The swimmers stare into the blaze. Behind the set features fear blooms. He walks out of the place with the captain of the garrison. When they are through the gate and into the darkness, his legs give way beneath him. He kneels on the cobblestones, shaking with the ague of his fate.

8

Cocalus is eating his breakfast on a balcony overlooking the sea. The storms have passed and the sun shines cheerfully. The king is in good spirits. He motions the stonecarver to a seat.

"Sit, sit. Do have an egg. Splendid eggs. Now, tell me how things are progressing."

He listens, peeling the shell from his egg, as the stonecarver lists times and places and possibilities. Cocalus nods.

"So, I'll keep King Cripple out of the way while they get rid of the captains. The palace guard aren't really up to this kind of thing, you know, killing people. They grow vegetables mostly. Life was quiet until you arrived. Does the storm follow you wherever you go? Mind you, it's quite bracing. Once in a while."

Cocalus begins to laugh, helplessly. It is the sound of misrule, chaos. He mops his eyes with a napkin. As his fit subsides, he says, "There is one thing though. Minos wants to see you. He speaks of nothing else. He wants to be sure he has the right man. Does he have the right man?"

Cocalus looks across the table. The stonecarver gives his thin smile.

"Minos is mad."

"He wants to see you, in chains, and when he sees you he wants your mouth bound shut. He is afraid even of the sound of your voice, it seems. Are you willing?"

Fear flowers in the stonecarver's bowels. He cannot know if this is betrayal he is being offered blandly at breakfast time. He wakes in the night, clammy with horror, from dreams of Minos' torturers.

"When?"

"This morning. It would have to be this morning."

Cocalus smiles indulgently and reaches for another egg.

9

"Thinner than I remember, smaller. This is him. This is my demon."

The stonecarver stands barefoot in the centre of the king's chamber under his load of chains, with a rope tied across his open mouth as if he were a beast.

"You are lucky, Cocalus. I have saved you from an evil fate. No doubt it seems strange to you. Just a man, you may think. You could break his bones, make him bleed, watch him die like any slave. But you would be wrong. Inside this envelope of flesh lives a devil, a destroyer. He brought chaos and destruction to my kingdom. He summoned up earthquakes and caused the entire island of Thera, with its cities and its people to sink beneath the sea. He caused the queen to give birth to a monster with the head of a bull. And then he flew away. He flew."

Cocalus catches the stonecarver's eye, raising his eyebrows faintly in a parody of alarm, Minos is circling him warily. He is quite mad. His dark staring eyes are never still. A tic flickers at the corner of his mouth. He turns to Cocalus.

"But I have mastered the demonic arts. I am a match for him now. See how I look into his eyes."

Minos is staring into the stonecarver's eyes. His face works uncontrollably, jerking and flinching. He comes toward him little by little, his arm reaching out, his fingers trembling.

"See how I touch him."

His face is a writhing mask and his thin woman's hand is shaking violently, but as he touches the captive's face, lays his palm along his cheek, the spasms subside, and he stands for a long moment staring uncomprehendingly into his eyes. Minos reaches round and gently unties the rope that is tied tight across the stonecarver's open mouth, leaving it looped around his shoulders.

"See me, Cocalus. See me."

His hands are holding the prisoner's face close to his own. He closes his eyes and kisses him slowly on the mouth.

Minos will never touch another human being. Already the fires are lit beneath the cauldrons in the room above his bath. Later, when the boiling water comes through the ceiling on to his naked body as he lies in the bath he will scream, and those that hear will never forget the sound. Minos will struggle free of the boiling deluge and die on the painted tiles. His sprawled, blistered, lobster red body will lie unattended through the night while his fleet burns. The blood will settle in blue lacunae in the catacombs of his corpse. The princesses will come down towards dawn, silently with a lamp, and they will kneel by the naked king, crooning and touching the chill, stone hard flesh.

10

The long swell rolls under the crowded fishing boats as they wait, a mile out from the fleet, waiting for the moon to set. The swimmers stand in silence in the wells of the boats with the fathomless sea passing beneath their feet. Someone coughs. A voice mutters nervously. Only the whites of their eyes show in soot blackened faces. The motionless moon goes down, sinking behind the unseen cliffs and starfields bloom overhead. The stonecarver watches the distant flicker as fires begin to take hold on the houses above the town. The game has begun. He touches the shoulder of the boatswain sitting on the bench next to him. There is a word and the oarsmen give way, pulling closer toward the fleet. There are four fishing boats. They pull way from one another as they make for their appointed places, shrinking into the stygian night. The lonely sound of oars, the creak and splash, fades to silence.

The stonecarver begins to make out the black shapes of the Cretan ships against the lights of the town. One of the swimmers, a slave, disappeared during the morning. No one knows anything. The possibility that they have been betrayed has occurred to everyone, and they will only know, when they come beneath the ships. The stonecarver has blacked his face and body. He will swim in the missing man's place. The anxiety that he is not a strong enough swimmer is merely another stratum on the bedrock of his fear, another question he does not know the answer to.

He touches the boatswain's shoulder and they give over. The boat loses way, rolling on the silent back of the sea. It is time to go, and there is a little surge of release among the men. The lamps are lit in the bottom of the boat where they burn like a little universe of tiny, wavering stars. The sacks are put over the side. They bob like tethered sheep. The men follow in twos, undressing and slipping naked into the dark swell, treading water, their gasping faces uplifted. The lamps are passed over and made fast to the tops of the sacks. The teams with the furthest to swim go first. He makes them take their time. He wants the fires to be started as near to the same time as possible. He fears for the latecomers when the alarm is raised. The last pairs disappear among the swellcrests and only he and the boy who is his partner remain. The rowers are resting at their benches. He leans down and speaks to the boatswain.

"Wait for me. These other lads are swimming to the shore when they've done. There will be crowds on the beaches, waiting to kill Cretans if they swim ashore. If they hear me shouting, with my Greek accent, they're bound to think I'm a Cretan. Show me a light when the fires have started."

He has a momentary vision of himself swimming and swimming in an empty black sea, unable to find the boat again. He puts his hand on the boy's shoulder. The youth is shaking violently and the man hugs him as if he were hugging a woman or a child, until he grows still. The stonecarver pulls his tunic over his head and sits for an instant on the bulwark, his bare feet in the cold water. The black water closes over him and he comes up gasping. The boy's head comes up next to him, and out of nowhere they grin at one another. The lamp is passed down from above and they make it fast to the top of the sack. They kick off, away from the boat and quite suddenly they are alone, paddling in silence, pushing their strange cargo up the long slopes of the swells. The town lights appear for a moment as they top each crest, and are lost again as they swoop into long shining troughs in which there is nothing but the kicking of feet. They toil through the hills of the sea, traverse the dunes of ocean. The youth is a strong swimmer and pushes the floating sack without effort. The stonecarver holds on to the rope from time to time and rests. Beneath them, a million motes of green phosphorescence drift like galaxies in the black, vertiginous deeps. In these fragments of time the stonecarver comes close to his quietus. In this simple labour, in this small bare journey across the face of the void, he feels nothing but the solace of effort, of absence.

High darkness looms to the left. Being the last to leave, theirs is the nearest galley. They turn in toward the tall shadow of the ship, kicking their feet with care, making no splash, no sound. They come beneath the black hull where the swell rises and falls against the tarred timber. There is a movement high up and they shrink against the ship, hearts pounding, thinking that they are betrayed. A pale arse swings out over their heads like a moon and a noisesome arc of liquid shit splatters into the water. There is a moan and a curse and a second arse appears, voiding into space. The stonecarver sees the boy's grinning teeth in his soot blackened face. They edge toward the stern. The steering oar rises out of the water like a tree and they push the floating sack into the space between it and the hull. It wedges tight and there seems no need to tie it in place. Holding on to the thickness of the steering oar in the rise and fall of the water, the stonecarver reaches up and removes the cowl from the lamp. The little flame burns bravely in the swooping darkness. He tips the lamp to one side and oil runs out, followed by a tiny snake of blue fire. The little flames gather and grow, evolving from blue to yellow. Oil has spilled down his forearm and a tongue of flame runs across the back of his hand and down his arm. He sinks down into the black water until only his face is above the surface, extinguishing the flames. The oil soaked sacking catches and long tongues of flame snake upward over the curving strakes of the hull. He sees the tar begin to blister. The boy is pulling at his arm and they swim away, out of the light. A hundred yards away a silent column of white flame spears upward, throwing the shape of another galley into precise relief. The stonecarver presses the boy's face between his hands for an instant. He points him toward the fires above the town and the boy grins before kicking away from him into the swell. The stonecarver treads water, watching the otter-slick glint of the boy's head as he tops each swellcrest, until he loses him altogether. Wherever he looks, pale vertical tongues of flame are beginning to flower on the dark back of the sea, but there is no noise yet, only a silence. He counts six, ten tongues of silent flame. He turns toward the open sea, swimming for the darkness, aware, as he rises to each swellcrest of the gathering light behind him. He turns again and waits a moment until the swell carries him up. The galleys are spread out like burning candles across the level horizon. He catches for the first time the remote sound of shouting.

He is far out now, very far from the burning forest. He feels seasick and he is cold. Though his limbs have grown leaden and he knows that he is nearly spent, the fatigue brings with it lassitude and a merciful indifference, so that he feels no anxiety, no fear. Turning on his back, he rests for a while in the lift and fall of the swell. He can see no sign of the fishing boat, no lantern light, but somehow it has become a matter of small importance. He cannot imagine seeing the light. The distant destruction seems remote, unconnected, and he finds no meaning in it, so he turns again and strikes out wearily for the last darkness.

11

A weight lifts from the youth as he swims away from the stonecarver. He is not afraid now. It comes to him that the danger is past and he is filled with elation. He is a strong swimmer and he can see, beyond the dark shapes of the fleet and the eels of fire which flicker here and there among the galleys, the houses burning on the hill above the town. He turns back for a moment and waves his arm in farewell, but he cannot see the king's man among the dark swells. Their ship is burning well now. A tongue of flame leaps vertically, high above the deck, illuminating the rigging and the mast. At last there is a movement on board. Figures gather along the bulwark. There is a scurrying and a shouting. The boy laughs out loud as he treads water, watching panic and confusion take hold.

At last he turns again for the shore. The black waters of the bay are alive with reflected firelight. To his left, another galley burns, its whole stern section an inferno. Fifty yards off, bobbing in the black water, the youth is mesmerised by the destruction. Silhouetted against the fierce glare, frantic figures move here and there like ants. Above the roar of the flames he can hear screams and urgent shouting. He sees a man jump from the deck and catches the faint white splash as he hits the water. He is followed by another and another.

In a moment the youth is alive again to himself and to his own danger. He looks around. Everywhere there are fires burning on the sea. He begins to swim again with powerful strokes, running the gauntlet of the burning ships, aware of the contained dread in his chest. The roar of the flames comes to him in surges as he tops each swellcrest. Ahead, the sea is burning everywhere. He makes his slow way past ships to left and right. They are the stuff of dreams, these burning galleys. The sky is coiled fire. Pale smoke and burning sparks drive like veils of strange rain across the infernal sea. Ruinous ships hang skeletally against the blinding glare of the firestorm.

He is aware of people in the water. Close to him, a voice is shouting. He cannot understand the words but the panic rises out of the sound, infecting him. He can see other swimmers ahead and beyond them he can see the fires above the town. He strikes out feverishly. To his left, shipmates struggle in the water. The one, unable to swim, is clutching and clawing his brother in his terror. His brother fights to get away. They thrash and scrabble, drowning together.

They are swimming in their hundreds now. He can see them all around him, making for the shore. He begins to detect the dim line of white where the waves are breaking along the beach below the town. Crowds of dark shapes are gathered along the water's edge. His feet find the bottom, steep shingle sliding away beneath him. Ahead, a Cretan staggers forward with his hands high in the air, crying words he does not understand. The youth begins to shout. It's all right! It's me! Friend! Friend! He is laughing and shouting, almost home.

Dark shapes advance toward the figure in front of him. An oar comes down like a club. The glint of a descending blade. The blows come down methodically. They wait upon one another, as if they were threshing corn. Everywhere in the seething shallows there are blows descending. Men and women, thigh deep in the suck of the shingle, are working like labourers with their oars and axes and cudgels. It is not a struggle but a harvest. The exhausted Cretans are going down dumb into the lace of the foam, like felled oxen. As far as the eye can see along that dim shore there are carcasses lifting and falling in the waves' backwash.

The boy sees a face he recognises. Two figures converge on the roaring youth as he slips and staggers forward, laughing and crying, to embrace his countrymen. The first blow falls across his shoulder so that he staggers to his knees, the shingle shifting beneath his feet. A dark wave lifts water into his mouth making him cough and retch. He reaches upward blindly as if he would clasp his assailant to him and the cudgel breaks his fingers as it descends upon his upturned face. He dies immediately from that second blow, though other blows follow. The corpse falls away and is dragged down the pebbles in the ebbing wave. It rolls in the restless shallows, in the heaving wrack.

12

"There!"

"Where? Where?"

"There, look, topping that sea!"

The boatswain stands up in the bow, his knees stiff, for he has been sitting a long while. They sat in the darkness to begin with, hanging over their oars, and there is nothing to see except the tiny glow of the burning houses in the town and they wonder whose houses they might be, though they are not overly concerned. All the houses at the top of the town belong to merchants, scribes, wealthy folk. And then the little spears of flame begin to appear here and there on the dark water. They start to count the separate fires as they bloom in the darkness: five: ten: twenty: twenty-two: twenty-four: shouting and pointing at each new shoot of flame, watching them gather and grow like flowers. The excited talk begins to falter and they fall silent in gathering awe. It seems that the whole bay is going up in flames. Tiny black silhouettes of galleys are etched on the great glow which stretches from horizon to horizon. Faint fragments of sound, hardly to be heard, come out of the distant inferno from time to time: the deep roar of the fires and other shriller noises. The boatswain lights a lantern and makes it fast in the bow of the boat. They begin to watch for the return of the king's man. They grow anxious as the time passes, craning into the night.

The boatswain stands and shouts through his cupped hands. He pauses, squinting into the black, and turns to the oarsmen in the well of the boat.

"Put about. Look lively now."

The oarsmen slide down into their places and the boat begins to turn as the oars dip. The boatswain is holding his lantern aloft. He is not sure he has seen anything. He peers over the bow, turning his head this way and that.

"Rest easy now."

The splash of the oars ceases, leaving only the soft slap of water against the strakes as the invisible boat rises and falls. He holds up the lantern. His strong sailor's voice calls across the empty night. He listens; they all listen. Nothing, only the easy slide of the dark sea swell. The boatswain stands intent. He does not want to lose the king's man to the sea. His will is fixed upon conjuring him out of the dim hills of the sea. Something. He cranes forward over the bow.

"Give way, my lads. Gently, gently."

He speaks softly to his men and the oars lift again. There! Something, something, a piece of driftwood, a man, something, on the rising flank of the swell twenty or thirty yards off. He shouts, holding the lantern high. There is no response.

"Larboard now. Steady, steady."

The bow eases round a little. They are nearer now, only a few yards off. It is a man. He does not see or hear them. It is the king's man, he is sure of it. The bow comes almost against the shoulder of the swimming man, looming over him, but still he is not conscious of it. The boatswain watches him for a moment. He is swimming with painful slowness, as if he were asleep. The boatswain leans down and catches him beneath his arm. The lead oarsman is next to him and together they haul him up and over the side, into the boat. He tumbles unresisting into the well, between the rowers' benches. They stare down at him. The light of the boatswain's lamp is in his eyes. He has the look of someone awakened from sleep and he flinches away from the light.

13

Sunless dawn. A chill wind blows off the empty waters of the bay. Figures move here and there on the long beaches. The women strip the corpses of their clothing. The naked bodies lie like fish, bluish, meaningless, waiting to be taken to the fires that burn along the shore. Fire and water. There are bleak ribald jokes. There is pleasure here, interest, in the stripping of a corpse, like washing clothes at the well. They speak of them, the corpses, as they might speak of fond and foolish children. It was always going to come to this. In the grey waves the men of the town work with their boathooks, dragging the bodies clear of the water. They lie half in and half out of the breaking waves, moving a little, so that you might imagine that they lolled at their ease in the shallows.

Out on the grey water there is nothing. Minos' fleet is no more. A handful of overcrowded galleys escaped, they say, sailing out of the bay in the first glimmer of dawn, past ships burning down to the waterline, bearing down over lost souls still swimming in the cold, alien waters. It is a poor and pitiable thing to die alone and far from home.

Cocalus the king is standing alone on the beach in the cold, dark wind, holding his heavy furs about him, watching the movement along the sea's edge. As far as he can see, there are people moving, like shades along the banks of the Styx, carrying their burdens, tending the fires. Black smoke rolls along the shore, close to the ground. The smell of burning is sickly, almost sweet, as if some unspeakable feast were being prepared.

A boat is moving toward the shore, a fishing boat, the oars lifting and dipping silently, as if it were a funeral boat. It comes into the beach. The rowers ship their oars and go over the side into the shallows, dragging the boat clear of the waves. Cocalus watches the stonecarver climb slowly out of the vessel. He stands like a refugee, huddled in a blanket, knee deep in the grey sea, taking in the scale of his handiwork.

Cocalus makes his way along the shore and stands a few yards above him on the steep wet shingle. The stonecarver turns his soot blackened face towards the king. His eyes are rimmed with red. He has the look of one returned from the dead. Cocalus is watching him.

"You look like the devil. Minos was right. You are a destroyer, a demon. Are you content with your night's work?"

The stonecarver stands shivering in his blanket for a long time, as if he had not heard.

"They never told me. I never knew. I used to make things, you know. I spent my life making things. I never questioned it. And then I killed Talos, the giant, and then I killed my own son. And now this. Who will judge me?"

Afterword

The story of Pasiphae, Daedalus and Minos is part of the common stock of Western Culture and unsurprisingly a number of other texts lie behind mine. Robert Graves' compendious *The Greek Myths* is a book I return to repeatedly. Anyone who felt moved to ferret amongst its arcane annotations would find an assortment of details which I have appropriated. Behind Graves' book lie the writings of Pausanias, Diodorus Siculus, Appollodorus and other Latin mythographers. (Many of these texts are readily available in translation through the Loeb Classical Library).

Behind these writers is the void. Somewhere beyond them lie the ur-narratives, that which is lost, and we can have no sense of how far back those narratives, written or spoken, might have taken us or how they have been made and remade in that lost past.

The story that I have engaged with has been reworked often. At the age of eighteen I read Michael Ayrton's *Testament of Daedalus* and was much impressed, though more perhaps by the drawings than by the text. I also tried unsuccessfully to read Ayrton's *The Maze Maker*. I think that elements of Mary Renault's *The King Must Die*, which I also read as a teenager, may have found their way into my own narrative though I have been careful not to read it since. As a child I read and reread an eerily illustrated copy of Charles Kingsley's *The Heroes*. Nothing precise remains in my memory of that book. What comes to me when I try to recall it is a sense of foreboding.

About 1500 BC the island of Thera which lies to the north of Crete exploded. What remains today is a caldera of volcanic debris filled by the sea. A few villages have grown up over the centuries on its precipitous rim. Near what is now the village of Akrotiri, a Minoan town was buried beneath the ash of that cataclysm. The archaeologist responsible for much of the early excavation of the site, Spyridon Marinatos, who died there beneath a falling wall, developed a hypothesis that it was the destruction of Thera which triggered the collapse of the Minoan palace culture on Crete. He pictured earthquakes, deluges of ash, tidal waves and a kind of universal trauma. Marinatos's theory has not been well received by historians but it provided me with a metaphorical subtext for the story of Pasiphae.

Other titles available from Dewi Lewis Publishing

Shortlisted for the 1998 Booker Prize

THE INDUSTRY OF SOULS
Martin Booth
£6.99, ISBN:1-899235-51-5

Arrested for spying in the early 1950s and presumed dead by the British Government, Alexander Bayliss, survives 20 years in a Soviet labour camp. Eventually freed, he has no reason to return to the West. Now, on his 80th birthday Russia is changed. Communism has evaporated and he must now make a choice, perhaps for the first time in his life...

'Beg, steal, borrow or buy this book. I'm not exaggerating, he really is that good.' – Sunday Star-Times, New Zealand

'His description of the death-trap mine is genuinely scary... a good read.' – Ian Thomson, The Daily Telegraph

'Booth's spare, unexaggerated style makes his description of Sosnogorsklag 32, the camp in which (Bayliss) is incarcerated, powerful and stark.' – Erica Wagner, The Times

❖ ❖ ❖

From the Winner of the 1999 London Writers' Award

DEPTH OF FIELD
Sue Hubbard
£8.99, ISBN:1-899235-82-5

Depth of Field is an acute observation of the nature of memory and identity. Having grown up with her Jewish identity submerged, Hannah experiences a deep sense of alienation. After her marriage falls apart she returns to London's East End in search of her roots and to work as a photographer. A failed affair, a breakdown, and a lost custody battle for her children, leave her alone to discover her own way to reconstruct her life.

'A very remarkable first novel.' – John Berger

'Lyrical, highly visual, beautifully observed.' – John Burnside

❖ ❖ ❖

MARTYLOVE
by Gary Waterman
£8.99, ISBN:1-899235-42-6

MARTYLOVE is a fast-moving, fast-talking, twentieth century, transatlantic tragi-comedy that follows the lives of three outrageous characters whose futures become inescapably and irredeemably entwined. Jane Miller, workaday English housewife, lives only for her pop star hero – Marty Moreno, the self-styled King of Smooch – who meanwhile crashes and burns towards an ignoble end in the Los Angeles fast-lane, a fate which only his minder, the ever-faithful Lance, can prevent. Bound together in an unholy triangle of secrets this is their story.

'Devastatingly original, energetic, visionary; the work of a genius.'
– Fay Weldon

'Funny, fast-moving, occasionally shocking, Martylove is a very welcome addition to literature's exploration of fandom. We've all been there.' – Alan Stewart, Amazon.co.uk

❖ ❖ ❖

RIDING ELECTRIC HORSES INTO THE VOIDS OF TIME
Alex Laishley
£8.99, ISBN:1-899235-28-0

Derek Alan Prosser – aka Arlo Hopewizer because, let's face it, if you're in the game, you need the name – is a child of the trans-Atlantic, silicon chip-based, imagino-centric techno-age. Late twenty-something, he's the millionaire owner and sole proprietor of BakTrax, Inc., an internationally famous and highly successful Computer Generated Entertainment company. Everything in his life is vintage millennium cool – London, his mews apartment, Zara, his Porsche Boxster. No longer snorting coke or rolling roaches, he is over his wild times…or is he? For, whilst Lucien, the style pundit, has finished fashioning his life, Addled Andy has moved from the mews and Nandy the Candy no longer sells him 'E' or 'ice', his world is about to take a bizarre turn.

❖ ❖ ❖

LAUGHTER IN A DARK WOOD
Peter Gilbert
£8.99, ISBN:1-899235-12-4

Driven by a humour which is both black and bittersweet, *Laughter in a Dark Wood* is an extraordinary and hilarious road movie of the mind. Bernard Steinway, an unemployed, isolated Jewish intellectual, attempts to find a sense of purpose in life following the collapse of his marriage. His search is both desperate and deluded as it moves from one self-inflicted disaster to another.

> 'Unceasingly witty and incisive… an exceedingly well written, wonderfully arresting debut.'
> The Times

'The best new book I've read this year. Darkly funny.'
Books Etc Staff Pick

'Splendid wit and verve.'
Martyn Goff

'Touching, funny, refreshingly retro... a truly original debut.'
Eva Hoffman

❖ ❖ ❖

THE LONG SHADOWS
Alan Brownjohn
£6.99, ISBN:1-899235-21-3

Set against the background of Thatcher's England and Ceausescu's Romania, Tim Harker-Jones, bequeathed the task of writing the biography of a famous novelist friend from the past, becomes involved in extraordinary intrigues that intertwine cultural ambition and political expediency. Skilfully crafted, beautifully written, the novel draws together a colourful cast-list of larger than life characters – cultural bureaucrats, eccentric anglophiles, dubious officials – all absorbed in the machinations of a totalitarian state moving uncertainly towards democracy; a society where truth is a commodity that is easily repressed and manipulated.

'A vivid insider's guide to the dark heart of Ceausescu's Romania... a literary thriller.'
Jonathan Coe, New Statesman

❖ ❖ ❖

For a full list of our publications please write to

Dewi Lewis Publishing
8 Broomfield Road
Heaton Moor
Stockport SK4 4ND

You can also visit our web site at

www.dewilewispublishing.com